MONTANA
Destiny

A Montana Romance

MONTANA
Destiny

A Montana Romance

VELDA
BROTHERTON

GALWAY

OGHMA CREATIVE MEDIA

www.oghmacreative.com

ISBN: 978-1-63373-237-7

Interior Design by Casey W. Cowan
Editing by Gil Miller

Galway Press
Oghma Creative Media
Bentonville, Arkansas
www.oghmacreative.com

To my friend and editor Gil Miller

*Thanks for all of your help, patience
and encouragement*

One

Across the sprawling valley patches of new grass shared space with winter-dried bare earth to form a crazy quilt. Purple mountains cut into a brilliant columbine sky. Along the ground clouds of dust moved in the wind like ghost herds pursuing the cattle drive. Mitch squinted into the bright spring sunlight. He was late. Spring roundup had begun.

Between his legs the powerful stallion shifted restlessly, nostrils flaring in a puff of wind. He held the animal yet another moment to absorb the intangible emotions that poured through him, hot, raw, and bittersweet. He'd never expected to return to Montana Territory. Yet the past that had kept him away had ultimately chased him back like an angry, wounded animal bent on revenge.

With an impatient grunt he settled the black Stetson firmly on his head, tilting it so the brim shadowed a scar that slashed through his left eyebrow. The vivid mark never let him forget what he had lost.

He shook off the memories. He'd come here to use his gun, and it was time he got to it. Long past time that someone paid for what had happened. Besides, the man who had hired him was waiting. No need to look back any longer. If he did he might catch sight of the beast that pursued him with such fury.

He loosened the reins. The black stallion neighed into the wind, tightened his haunches, and tore down the incline.

Most of that day Mitch rode across Circle D land until at last he reached the colonel's house, a rambling, low structure squatted on high ground at the horseshoe bend of Little Porcupine Creek. Before dismounting, he rested a moment to study the enormous ranch house, its extravagant glass windows, the wide veranda skirted by freshly dug flower beds. At last he dropped wearily from the horse and pulled a leather gun belt and holster from his saddlebag. Without removing the black cowhide gloves he strapped on the Colt .44 and settled it low so the gleaming butt rested a trifle below his right hip.

Charlie rode easy in the saddle and let the roan work the milling longhorns. The tough little mare deftly turned the cows and calves and headed them back in the direction of the branding camp. Other cow hands rode in, all herding cattle from their assigned sections.

The rowdy exuberance of spring roundup chased away Charlie's winter doldrums. She grinned broadly. Grains of dust gritted between her teeth and she uncapped a canteen to rinse her mouth and take a long swig. The bawling and bellowing, the cracking of the cattle's horns as they clashed, the pounding of hoofs, were as sweet as first light after a cold night on the trail.

For the first time since her father died, she felt good! The long boring winter of grief and utter, complete isolation behind her, Charlie actually looked forward to life in this new country. She would have to be tough as nails to make it without her father, for Matthew Houston had truly been the strength of the Double H Ranch.

"We'll call it the Double H," he'd said, "for the two Houstons." And then he'd grinned at her and rumpled her hair, the closest he ever came to showing affection.

Could she hold on and fulfill his dream here in this wild and vast country? Its merciless conditions tested the endurance of even the hardiest man. Even so, she enjoyed the turmoil of roundup, the feel of the roan shifting and dancing between her knees, the sweat trickling down her backbone as the sun climbed the sky. The dirt, the smell, the aching muscles. All glorious. And she wouldn't think of Matt's tragic death today. Fury always came on the heels of such thoughts, and she was weary of being angry. Winter had been the time for mourning; spring was for celebration of this new life.

She leaned forward and urged Belle closer to the bunching cattle, laughing aloud at the antics of a calf lumbering awkwardly in a halfhearted gallop after its mother, tongue hanging from the side of its mouth dribbling with foam.

A Rocking R puncher whooped and charged his pony in a wide circle to corral an escaped steer, and Charlie could contain her pleasure no longer. With an answering shout she swept off her worn Stetson. The wind twisted through her cropped hair, cut short like a man's so that the black curls just touched her shoulders.

The herd circled and milled, and she reined up to let the expert cutters begin their exhausting work of roping the calves and dragging them to the flankers for branding.

"Dammit, Matt, we made it," she cried. "We got through the winter. How do you like that, by God, just how the hell do you like that?" She squeezed her eyes shut, willed away moisture that gathered there, and swallowed the thick lump in her throat.

She pulled herself away from the brink of grief. She mustn't let go. Not now, not ever.

After a filling meal from the chuck wagon, she rested on her haunches and listened to the tally from the branding fire.

Neighboring rancher Cal Malone settled in beside her, picking up a stick to doodle in the dust between his scuffed boot toes.

"We made 'er, Charlie, we surely did," he said, and traced a gigantic *X* in the dirt for emphasis.

She glanced at her friend and nodded. Lingering smudges under his eyes told of his own grief last winter. Maybe that's why they had gravitated toward each other like they had.

"Glad to see spring, Cal, I surely am."

He gazed out across the sprawling countryside and breathed deeply. "Wish Becky could... well, you know she loved the springtime. But then, who could blame her? Winters in Montana ain't no picnic." Cal sniffed and rubbed at his nose. "Aw, hell. Anyway, how you think you did?"

Charlie knew the question didn't call for a specific answer, it was just trail talk. Until the tally was done they'd neither one have any idea how their herds had fared over the winter.

"Well, Cal, they say it was a mild winter. Being from Texas I wouldn't know, but I'll tell you one thing. If thirty below for two weeks at a time is mild, I'm dreading the tough ones."

Cal laughed, "Well, hell, gal. Two weeks ain't nothing. I've seen it forty below for a month or more, forty inches of ice and snow and a wind straight off the pole."

"Yeah, yeah, Cal. I've heard the stories."

The two chuckled comfortably. Of all the ranchers, Cal treated Charlie the most fairly. It was like he knew she was a woman and allowed for that, but yet figured her to do just about anything she set her mind to without qualification.

They had another bond too, one that no one else knew about. Cal wrote poetry and Charlie made up music for the words. Of all things, they'd discovered their similar inclinations at the gathering after Rebecca's funeral the previous October.

Neither of them ever discussed it much, the poetry and music nonsense, like maybe they were a bit embarrassed by it even though they couldn't seem to stop the creating. Every once in a while Cal would hand Charlie a wrinkled piece of brown paper with a poem scribbled on it, words crossed out and rewritten, some nearly illegible, and the next time they met she'd sing him the words, and neither of them able to read a note of music.

"Gawd, don't that smell like money?" Cal said, and pointed with the stick toward the buzz of activity around the branding fire.

As the brander shouted out the mark a calf's mother carried, the iron tender would fetch that particular branding iron from those lined in the fire. Too hot meant a bad blister on the calf's hide, not hot enough meant the brand would likely hair over and become indistinct. Few mistakes were made, for these men were all experts at what they did.

"They're calling twenty Circle Ds to every Double H or Rocking R, though." She inhaled the stench of burned hair, grimaced at the fearsome bawling of the calves when the cherry-red iron sizzled their hides.

"That's okay. The colonel, he's got a spread the size of one of them eastern states. Bound to have more cattle than us."

Before it was finished the joint roundup would cover several hundred square miles and encompass the grazing land of more than half a dozen ranches. And it was true the Circle D belonging to Colonel Hulbert P. Dunkirk was immense, much of it gained by devious means. Still, they'd all work together, it was the only way in this majestic and demanding territory where one mishap could mean death.

Contemplating death made her think of Matthew, even though she tried not to. What a dreadful memory, watching powerless and grief-stricken as they lowered her father's canvas-wrapped body into a muddy grave alongside the trail near Ogallala last fall. Nebraska Territory was a far piece and those heart rending days long behind her. It made her angry that she couldn't bury the worst of the memories and keep only the best.

She tried by joshing with her friend. "Well, hell, Cal, there's another Double H calf."

He grinned.

She was happy to see that. He'd taken his wife Becky's death real hard, especially since their baby had not lived either. He was mighty alone, and she hoped someday he'd find himself another woman. Good women, though, were as scarce in this territory as were the conveniences that attracted them.

She rose and stretched, standing still to enjoy the sun's warmth through her shirt as she raised both shoulders and rolled her head backward to loosen some of the kinks.

"Double H," the brander shouted again.

Smiling, she screwed the bedraggled hat back onto her head, then turned sharply at the rattle of horses' hooves approaching from the southwest.

"Who in thunder is that?" Cal asked, coming to his feet.

Together they shaded their eyes and squinted into the bright white glare.

"Looks like that bastard of a colonel," she said. "Wonder what brings him out here?"

"Got an army with him. What you reckon he's up to?"

She figured whatever the colonel had in mind boded no good. Colonel Dunkirk, a man of reasonable girth, rode in a fancy carriage drawn by a white horse, and he reined in near the rope corral where the extra horses were tied. He wore what appeared to be a military uniform. She knew it wasn't. He ordered his wardrobe in Miles City and the style signified nothing but his ego. Flanking him on either side were more than half a dozen gun hands, men hired not to herd cattle or do any ranch work, but to ride roughshod over smaller ranchers so that sooner or later Colonel Dunkirk would own all they had.

Because Circle D was the biggest spread, Dunkirk's ramrod, a fellow by the name of Bodwell, was running the wagon for this roundup. He bossed the riders, his own and the smaller ranchers', with a harsh fist. Charlie had tried not to dislike the bully of a man, but it wasn't easy. He treated her as if she didn't exist, assigning duties without so much as a glance at her. She was left to pick her own jobs, which she did without comment. He deserved a good punch in the mouth, and she figured she might give it to him if he didn't watch out.

"Well, he sure as hell never rides out to roundup," Cal said. "Not since I've been here. Let's go see what's up."

The colonel acknowledged Cal, another rancher by the name of Duffy McGrew who owned a spread up on the Missouri, and the Double H ramrod Yancey Barton. His eyes wandered to Charlie and he touched the brim of his hat with two fingertips.

She sucked in a frustrated breath. "Surprised to see you out here, Colonel." Red anger flashed through her good humor.

He didn't meet her gaze, but stared out across the prairie. "Why wouldn't I be? My interest in this roundup is a hundred fold more than any of yours." He waved a doeskin-gloved hand to include the other ranchers.

"Depends entirely on how you look at it," Cal Malone said.

Charlie nodded curtly in her rancher friend's direction, and as she swung her attention away the agitated movement of a long-legged black stallion caught her attention. Eyes rolling wildly, nostrils flaring, the magnificent animal pranced into view from behind the colonel. On the stallion's back sat a man every bit as untamed in appearance as his mount. This was no cowhand, nor was he an ordinary gun hand. Back ramrod-straight, long legs taut in the stirrups, he gave the impression of a predator stalking prey. The way he sat his horse reminded her of the *vaqueros* in the paintings in her grandparents' home in south Texas. Men who were cowboys long before this country knew the meaning of the word. Proud, stalwart, mysterious. There the resemblance ended. His eyes, as green as the deep summer woods on a stormy day, were fathomless and frosted like crystals. They registered nothing, even though his glance flicked over each of the ranchers in turn. He wore a pistol slung low on his right hip and carried a rifle in his scabbard. The black stallion never stopped its restless motion, and the man's body moved lithely to compensate.

After a moment he noticed her studying him and tipped his hat back away from his face to get a better look. A jagged pale scar cut upward from his left eyebrow into a streak of white in the black hair. His expression remained as stoic as a finely hewn statue. Her skin prickled like it did when a sudden thunderstorm approached.

Dunkirk cleared his throat loud enough to get everyone's attention. "Just wanted to introduce all of you to my new man, in case you run across him on the range. This here's Mitchell Fallon, he's my rep, come to help me keep a tally. He'll make sure none of you small ranchers overstep your bounds and burn a few brands where they don't belong."

Charlie's loosely reined temper flared. She tightened her lips and kept her eyes hard on the colonel. "If anyone is likely to do that, sir, it's you and your collection of ratty gunfighters."

Mitch gave the brash cowpoke a second look. On first glance, he'd thought her a young man, but now saw she was a rough and hardened female who looked like a good scrubbing wouldn't hurt her any. Damn shame, considering the shortage of good-looking women, for this one to choose to go as a man. But what the hell? It made him no difference. If he came up against her, he'd treat her just like all the rest and do what he'd been hired to do.

He rode for a brand, he honored it. Suited him fine that Colonel Dunkirk had a dark craving to rule this land. To the strongest and meanest go the spoils. Mitch didn't much care, one way or the other, who came out on top. This was a job that suited his temperament; it gave him plenty of excuse to get back at men who deserved to pay for what had happened to him.

The colonel ignored Charlie's comment.

Of course, that only made her angrier and mouthier. "As for your hired hand, keep him and his kind off my ranch. I may be new up here and I may be a woman, but don't make any mistakes you'll regret. I don't intend to lose my land to thieves and killers."

Despite her anger Charlie couldn't take her eyes off the man in black who gazed right past her as if she didn't exist. Though he appeared to be paying no attention to his immediate surroundings, he held his right arm slightly bent, hand almost touching the pistol. Dunkirk had been heard to vow more than once that he would own all of Montana's grazing land one day. And this man was here to help him do just that. He was a gunslinger, pure and simple. The way Dunkirk accumulated land was nothing short of stealing. Even if he did give it a fancy name like possessory rights, it was still illegal.

Yancey Barton slid to her side, said under his breath, "We don't need the likes of him, but if I was you I wouldn't rile him."

"You don't have to rile a man like that. He comes riled. Besides, it looks to me like we don't have a choice," Charlie whispered back to her ramrod.

The man in black startled her by belatedly acknowledging Dunkirk's introduction in a voice hard-edged and emotionless. "I'll be around."

Abruptly he met her gaze with a calculating expression that gave her the shudders right down to the depths of her soul. She had never feared any man or beast in her life, but this man's lifeless tone and granite stare were terrifying in a way she couldn't explain. Her mouth dried and her heart paused in its beating. Whatever she might have been about to say to Yancey or Cal, or for that matter the colonel, evaporated. She turned on her heel and fled the confrontation. As she untied Belle she noticed her fingers were trembling. A familiar, unwanted sensation settled in the pit of her stomach, like some long-lost desire no longer recognized. Her reaction to the man terrified her even more than he himself had.

Yancey sat beside Charlie that evening while they were eating. He didn't say much until both had finished off their plates of beans and biscuits, but she knew he had something on his mind.

"The man's gonna take all the land, Charlie, and I don't see a way in hell we can stop him. It's just a matter of time."

She sipped at her coffee and stared off across the campfire at the lone figure of Mitchell Fallon. He had backed up under a tree and lit a thin black cheroot. In the dark he might have been staring at her, she couldn't tell.

Swiftly she turned her attention to Yancey. "What would Matt do?"

"Fight, I reckon. He always did."

"But he had Richard King to back him up. The most powerful rancher in Texas. When you have friends like that you don't have to do too much fighting."

"Did to get where he was though, same as King. You don't think someone handed him that spread in Santa Gertrudis on a platter, do you?" Yancey tossed the dregs of his coffee to the ground.

"You telling me to fight, Yancey? Is that what you're telling me? And if so, will you and the men back me?"

The ramrod studied her for a long moment, squinting his blue eyes so that the sun-wrinkled skin folded in around them. "Ain't no place for a woman, fighting for a spread."

"Don't you dare tell me that, Yancey Barton. Every woman who takes up with a rancher fights for the life as much as her man does. She wears herself out fighting." Hot tears stung her eyes and she turned quickly away, not wanting him to see. Dammit, she had to be tougher than this.

"Now, sweetheart, don't go getting touchy on me. You know blamed well what I meant. Nobody knows better than me how hard you've worked, or any rancher's wife, for that matter.

"It's just you don't have no business going up against men like *that* un—" he gestured toward Fallon "—with a six-shooter in your hand. He'll win 'cause he's meaner, not 'cause you're a woman, and that's a fact."

She sighed and drank the last of her coffee. "Then what do I do? Hire someone like him?"

"Well, there's that, and—" Yancey stood and looked down at her. "—or we could band together, you and the others Dunkirk wants to force out. Go to the law about his thievin ways."

She snorted. "Nobody cares that he rookered a bunch of war widows out of their land-bonus privileges, or that every man in his outfit has filed a claim and signed it over to him. Sheriff Newton turned a blind eye to the vigilantes who strung up those homesteaders a while back. Dunkirk found them squatting on his land and that was all that mattered. And what about poor Ruell Denver? Just happened to be unlucky enough to ride up on some bad doin's and ended up getting blamed for rustling and strung up. What makes you think a man of Sheriff Newton's caliber, lawman or not, would help us?"

"Well, gal, then I reckon you have to go higher than the sheriff. Contact the territorial governor or a marshal."

Charlie stood and stretched. The idea didn't appeal to her. Ride all over hell and creation chasing some politician who would have no inkling what was really going on out here even after she explained it. No, sir, she was a rancher not a crusader, but maybe Yancey did have something in suggesting that the small ranchers band together. Once the roundup was over she would speak to Cal and Duffy about it, see what they thought. There was that Englishman Hawthorne east of the colonel's and Les Burns whose place laid alongside of Duffy's, and a couple more whose names she hadn't learned yet, even though their cows had turned up at the branding fire.

That night, asleep in her bedroll until time for her watch, Charlie dreamed of the man in black with the snowy streak in his hair. Sensual perceptions brought her awake with that all too familiar deprived ache deep inside, and it was a long time before she went back to sleep. She had dreamed of him satisfying those needs in a most unthinkable way, and it disturbed her deeply.

The man in black was certainly not to be desired, even if she harbored such thoughts, which she didn't. She had played the role of her father's son too long to even consider such feminine longings. At twenty-six she was a confirmed spinster, and that was the way she wanted it. She relegated the dream to the place of nightmares where she stored memories too painful to deal with.

Yancey roused her for the early morning shift two hours before dawn. Though most cowboys disliked pulling guard at that hour, she preferred it. It meant that she would be in the saddle longer than those who had drawn guard duty during the night, but it was an even swap considering the quiet beauty of the predawn hours.

Still only half-awake she swung into the saddle and settled easily while the compact quarter horse plodded slowly around the perimeter of the sleeping cattle. Belle too knew her job. After a while Charlie began to hum, softly at first, then louder. The cows liked singing and whistling, it kept them settled down, just as it had during the long arduous drive up from Texas. Roundup was little different from that six-month cattle drive, it just didn't last quite so long. In two or three weeks they'd be finished with the branding and could settle back to normal ranch tasks until fall roundup in August when beeves would be cut out for shipping to market. By then yearlings would have fattened on the lush, green summer grasses and would bring a good price.

She let her clear voice rise to meet the gentle night wind, singing the ballad of Lasca, a favorite of all cowboys.

"Lasca used to ride on a mouse-gray mustang, by my side."

Across the way someone began to accompany her on a mouth harp. Off to her left creek water murmured over its rocky bed, adding to the melody.

"She was as bold as the billows that beat. She was as wild as the breezes that blow."

As she continued the song, Charlie thought she heard the steady thud of horses' hooves out of cadence with those of her own mount. She broke off the stanza and listened intently, but there was nothing but the soughing of the wind through treetops and the sweet song of the harp blending with the rush of water. Off and on during the hours before the sky lightened to silver, and long after she finished the heartbreaking tune with "Does half my heart lie buried, there, in Texas, down by the Rio Grande?" the prickly sensation that she was being watched wouldn't go away. Still she saw no one.

Mitchell Fallon reined in his horse abruptly. He had been so caught up in the singing that he had almost ridden up on a rider skulking along in the shadows. The man appeared to be following someone, but in the dark Mitch couldn't tell who. The rider continued to give that impression by moving in furtive stops and starts.

The singer halted for a moment, so did Mitch and so did the mysterious rider. After a while the woman began to sing again, a tune that plucked at Mitch's heart. He could practically hear tears in the voice as he made out the sad tale of lovers caught up in a stampede and the woman dying in her lover's arms.

Buried emotions rose in his chest and he used anger to suppress them. What in the hell was he doing out here in the middle of the night in the first place? It sure wasn't to listen to some corny love song. The colonel had said he should be visible, keep an eye on things, get to know faces and habits so he would be useful later when the man put into action his strategy for getting rid of these small ranchers.

Deliberately Mitch rode out into the open so that the rider he was pursuing could see him, and shouted a noncommittal greeting that came out more like a grunt. The cowboy replied with a similar sound and Mitch rode on.

Even when he did bed down he couldn't sleep. The strains of the beautiful and forlorn ballad haunted him, and he knew Charlie Houston was responsible. Her and her ebony dark eyes that wouldn't leave a man alone. It was unnerving to catch sight of her watching him. He wanted nothing to do with a woman, especially not one who was supposed to be his enemy. So why was he lying awake in the dark of night thinking about her? He turned one way, then another, but each time he closed his eyes, there she was asking something provocative and dangerous of him.

Finally he rolled from his blankets and, carrying his boots, crept out of camp. He wore no shirt and a ripple of cool air off the water sent goose bumps skittering over his bare flesh. At the edge of the creek he sat on a large boulder and gazed east across the shadowy plains that rose gently toward the sky.

In his heart, his dead wife cried softly, and he could find no way to quiet her. The presence of the Houston woman had reawakened his guilt, and that made him angry. There were times when he simply wanted to ride to the edge of a cliff and dive off, join Celia and their child and be done with facing day after endless day with the unanswered question on his lips. Why hadn't the men who had senselessly killed his wife and child killed him too? He had asked it thousands of times, but there was only silence in reply. The absence of reason nagged at him like a forgotten lyric, a faded dream.

Stars winked in the flowing water and he thought again about killing the men who had so brutally murdered his family. For a long while that was all he'd thought about, but he wasn't a killer, never had been, despite the reputation he'd gained after the war. A war did its best to turn a man mean, and Lord knows that one had, but his outlaw ways had been aimed more at something else. Taking back what should have been his. Payback for having been robbed of his family and his life. He had never returned home to his parents and sister in Missouri, and he blamed the war for that too.

Dear God, how he wished things had been different

During the next few days the roundup chewed away the

miles in a slow, distinct rhythm. Riders fanned out into the brushy hills to bring in strays. Men returned covered in mud after rescuing some unlucky animal trapped in a bog. At night exhausted cowboys who had been in the saddle up to eighteen hours snored loudly through a few hours rest. The days became one long blur of backbreaking work that left everyone worn out come bedtime.

Occasionally Charlie caught sight of the gunslinger, but never so that she was forced to acknowledge his presence. He paid little attention to her at all, and it humiliated her to be caught a couple of times staring at him. She did notice that he didn't pull guard and only occasionally rode herd. He was simply there and everyone walked a wide circle around him. He ate alone, rode alone, slept apart from the others like a renegade wolf wary of the pack.

Despite all that, something in his demeanor beckoned to her, made her wish she knew more about him. She wanted to speak to him, to discover what attracted her, but she dare not, for he was the enemy.

Two

Ever since Charlie had first drawn nighthawk duty she'd had a sense of being watched, but could never catch anyone in the act. It didn't make sense anyway.

Why would anyone want to follow her around?

Still, the feeling persisted and she kept a wary eye out. The roundup was winding down, going into the last few days as the circling riders scouted out the last of the scattered cattle, when she finally caught the man.

That evening she drew early night watch. Under the roan's hooves the ground grew dark quickly, but the night sky shone silver, silhouetting trees and cattle and riders. She let the mare wind lazily around the stragglers yet to be branded. Most of the cows, newly branded calves, castrated steers, and bulls had been released to the vast summer pastures, and the evening was hushed and placid.

From off to her right came the deep-throated cough of a resting animal. She glanced at the dark humps settling down for the night. That's when she distinctly heard the rattle of a horse's hooves in creek gravel where no one needed to be riding. Digging her heels into the roan's flanks, she reined her off in the direction of the sound and nearly rode into Ritter, a green hand she had hired just for the roundup.

Brown eyes wide in a youthful face, he looked ready to spook when he recognized her.

She pulled up, spoke harshly, "What are you doing out here?"

Ritter clawed his hat off his head. Hair stuck up like patches of straw. "Sorry, ma'am. Just looking... just checking... oh, lawd."

"Don't call me *ma'am*, my name is Charlie Houston. Pick one, or even Miss Houston, but not *ma'am*."

"No, ma'am... uh, no, sir... dang it all."

"What's wrong with you?" She glared at the stammering young man, trying to remember why she had hired him. He appeared to be totally inept, this lean-jawed youth who wore a hat so big it rested on his ears, but she couldn't recall watching him work. "Have you been following me around, Ritter?"

He clutched the hat to his chest, then turned it in rawboned hands too large for the rest of him. No answer came.

"Well?"

"Well?" he echoed. "No— I mean, I suppose." He gulped noisily. "Yes, ma'am," he bellowed so that Charlie's horse twitched and laid back its ears.

In the herd several cows bawled, horns rattled together. Her shoulders hunched. "Keep your voice down. Want to start them stampeding? Where in thunder did you work before you came here? Couldn't have been on a cattle ranch. And tell me again why I hired you."

"Up north around the Marias. I was a jingler."

Charlie snorted, still unable to recall what weakness had caused her to put this young man on the payroll.

"Isn't any wonder you're green," she said. A jingler was the lowest man on the roundup. He saw to herding the remuda and keeping up with all the saddle horses, but he also drew all the dirty chores, like rustling wood and water for the cook, peeling potatoes, and helping set up and tear down camp. Jobs no respectable cowboy would undertake, no matter what.

She slanted a hard glance at him. "Even a jingler manages to learn something. How long did you work for them?"

Ritter dropped his chin down on his chest and muttered into it "Last fall was my first. My pap was a farmer."

"A sodbuster. Your first was last fall? And tell me, Ritter, did you think that one of your duties when I hired you on at the Double H was to spy on me?"

He ducked his head. "No, ma'am."

"Well, then, why in thunder...." She sighed to calm herself. "I don't even remember including you on this roundup. If I remember right, I left you back at the ranch to lend a hand where you were needed. So tell me, Ritter, what in thunderation are you doing skulking around like some hyena?"

"Mr. Barton—he said I should, I mean, he thought—"

"Barton put you up to this? Yancey?" She trusted her ramrod as if he were an older brother and he put this greenhorn on her tail. Yancey had been by her father's side since the day Matt went out on his own to start the Double H when the War Between the States ended in '65. How dare Yancey set some snot-nose like Ritter on her trail to watch over her. Who did he think he was?

Charlotte Houston was four years old when Matt Houston took her from her Mexican grandparents and their palatial home and moved onto the King Ranch in Texas. He was ranch foreman there, and considered he'd made a place at last for his motherless daughter after years of trying to start his own spread.

She didn't remember her mother, and until the day her father came for her, Charlie, then called Charlotte by her extended Mexican family, spoke only Spanish, wore beautiful dresses and shiny patent leather shoes, and was doted upon by grandparents and a large number of aunts, uncles, and cousins.

Nowadays Charlie could speak no more than a few words of her mother's language, in fact did not even remember living with her grandparents. Since her father's death she'd experienced flashes of memory, mostly during the dreaded hours when she awoke in the middle of the night and could not go back to sleep.

When she was fifteen Matt went out on his own with King's blessing and some prize stock that included a few head of the newly bred quarter horses of which King was so proud. Charlie began to work beside her father as if she were his son. Together they built a ranch in Texas that, while it never rivaled the mammoth King spread, was something of which to be proud.

Then along came the cattle glut and the recession that spawned Matt Houston's dream. He'd heard about the cattle drives to Montana and the lush grassland just going begging, and he began to plan for the day when he would drive his longhorns the 1,500 miles into central Montana and build a barony of his own. So in the spring of 1875 Matt and Charlie Houston, along with Yancey Barton, seventeen faithful hands, and Chocco the cook, left Texas and headed north.

Charlie had never faltered in her duties, not even when Matt was killed, and now here stood one of her green hands telling her that her trusted ramrod had actually ordered him to spy on her. She'd be damned if she'd put up with that, not even from Yancey Barton.

"You ride in my place, Ritter."

"Me, ma'am?" He gulped, too late trying to swallow the forbidden form of address.

She tugged Belle's head around, bumping Ritter's mount and sending it dancing. "That's what I said, and I am the boss, not Yancey Barton. You got that, boy?"

"Yes'm, I do," he stammered.

The horse was surefooted in the dark or Charlie would

have been pitched to the ground as she urged the roan back to camp where she dismounted and stomped her way through the sleeping men until she came upon Yancey Barton's still form.

Stripping back the bedding, she grabbed her foreman by the shirtfront and yanked him to a sitting position.

He peered at her owlishly. "What in the *hell*…? Charlie. Damn, what's happened, girl? You all right? You hurt? What…?"

"You put Ritter on me, and I want to know why," she demanded, anger throbbing at her temples like thunder.

Yancey closed his hands around her balled fists that still clutched his shirtfront. "Take it easy, sweetheart. Lord, I thought something god-awful had happened. Ritter?"

"The young greenhorn. He's been following me around, says you put him up to it."

The man lying in the bedroll next to Yancey rolled over. "What the hell's going on? Can't a feller get some sleep? Dang."

"Can't we talk about this in the morning, Charlie?" Yancey said in a low voice.

"No, we're talking about it right now."

"Well, I don't understand why you're so all-fired mad, I was just doing my job like Matt told me to."

Charlie squeezed her eyes shut and gritted her teeth. "Matt's dead. Dead. And I'm running the outfit. You don't… dammit, you don't just do something like that. I intend to see to Matt Houston's dream, and I don't need some snot-nosed kid sneaking around keeping an eye on me, and I sure don't need you putting him up to it. You work for me, you got that?"

An anger such as she had never experienced came over Charlie, so that she fled from Yancey before she could give vent to it. Cursing under her breath, she stomped her way through the bundles of sleeping, weary cowboys.

Charlie shoved through the double swinging doors of the Powder Keg, took a quick look around, and spotted Cal at the bar. Ignoring a few greetings she elbowed through the crowd of celebrating hands.

He spotted her coming. "Buy you one, Charlie?"

"If the next one's on me."

Cal Malone chuckled. "I reckon that'll be okay."

He signaled Lance, who owned the place and tended bar when he couldn't get anyone else to take the job. The well-fed man laid a meaty palm over the two bits Cal slapped down for the drinks.

Lance eyed Charlie, for ladies weren't allowed in the bar. He had put up with her before, and a glance from Cal told him to do so again. Charlie grinned. She appreciated Cal as a friend. He took her at face value.

They talked about the tally, how each ranch had done, and drank the foamy brew. Charlie was comfortable with Cal, even when he criticized her choice of beeves. Cal favored Durhams and shorthorns and had begun to breed them into his herd. It wasn't an argument, simply a discussion, and things were calm, considering the crowd, when someone bumped Cal's elbow and dumped his mug of beer down the front of his shirt.

The rancher's short temper flared. He roared, slammed the mug down hard on the bar, and swung around with big fists cocked to take full measure of his adversary.

Even though he had to look up at the man who had bumped him, Cal didn't back down. He was set to pop him one. He'd been like that since Becky and the baby died, and Charlie guessed she understood, but when she caught sight of Mitchell Fallon's flat agate gaze she grabbed Cal's arm. It did no good.

The iron-hard muscles flexed, shaking her loose, and Cal came around in a swing headed for Fallon's jaw. The gunfighter dodged the punch much like a snake striking. His head wasn't in the line of fire anymore, and it was so quick that Cal, expecting to hit something solid, went stumbling past Fallon and into the crowd around the bar.

Before Cal could make his way back through the men who were doing their best to hold him off for fear the gunman would shoot him, Charlie and Mitchell Fallon sort of stumbled into each other.

She put her hands flat against his chest and pushed away. "Want to hit me too?"

"Haven't hit anyone yet. Son of a bitch comes back I'll wipe up the floor with him. Got a quick temper for a little man. Could get him killed."

She narrowed her eyes to slits. "You watch out who you threaten, Mr. Fallon. You may work for Colonel Dunkirk, but that doesn't give you free rein around here. If I were you I'd drink someplace else. Someplace where you're welcome."

"I drink where I please, and I work for who I please. Never have asked anyone's permission for either. And don't think because you're a woman you can talk to me like I'm filth. I got as much a right in here as you do."

The rigid tone of his voice, the angry clench of his strong jaw, hit her like a physical blow. He had remained the distance from her that she had created with her earlier shove, but she swore she could feel the fire of his breath aimed at her.

Caught up in his unfaltering gaze, she lifted her chin and squared both shoulders, though inside she trembled so hard she just knew he could see her jittering.

Faced down like that by a woman, Fallon's austere expression softened, and for just the flickering of an instant she saw in his features a sadness so intense that it overwhelmed the harsh demeanor. Before she could be sure, and before she could respond to the encounter, he had shoved past her and out of the saloon. She was surprised to feel a thick lump in her chest, an aching loneliness. Sometimes she missed her father so much it was unbearable, and at such inopportune times. It annoyed her that a run-in with that frightful man could be such a moment. Matt could have dealt with this situation and smoothed the waters in such a way that both men would have gone away feeling vindicated. She guessed she'd inherited her emotions from her mother's family.

She shared another beer with Cal, but both were so upset by the encounter with the gunslinger that they parted company. Cal, she supposed, would find a pretty girl and love his way out of his foul mood in one of the cribs out back. She decided to ride on home to the ranch. Night riding was one of her favorite pastimes especially when she needed settling.

As she headed out of Miles City on the surefooted roan darkness crept across the azure sky, stealing lazily from east to west to swallow the flaring sunset. By the time she topped the rise above the ranch the vast sky was a deep purple awash with millions of stars. She halted there a moment, visualizing more than seeing the ranch buildings spread out below her. Not much yet. Not much.

"It's your dream, Matt. Dammit, why couldn't you stick around to make it come true?" As the spoken words tumbled into the empty night she stared through tears at the flickering stars.

She ought to just ride away, leave behind the marauding Indians, the prowling wolves, and the two-legged snakes who would like to see her fall. Just go back to Texas and her mother's people where she could learn to be a lady.

Between her legs the restless pony tossed its head and

whinnied, danced a little two-step. She came out of her reverie, rubbed at the tight muscles along the animal's tawny neck. "Ho, boy. Ho. What's wrong?"

A replying whinny came out of the nested darkness below. The horses penned in the corral back of the skeleton of a barn moved restlessly, their hooves thudding.

In that instant she saw something flash inside the raw log walls of the roofless structure, and nudged her heels into the mare's belly to ride a bit closer. Flames erupted in the doorway of the barn and out of the inferno burst a horse and rider. Columns of fire leaped into the sky as the animal raced across the barnyard. She skinned her Winchester from its scabbard and without aiming pulled off several shots at the fleeing figure, hunched low in the saddle. She couldn't really see him except in the fierce glow of the fire, and the surrounding darkness quickly engulfed him.

Maybe she'd hit him, maybe not.

She vaulted to the ground and raced for the water trough. A sickness down inside told her it was no use. What little water she could haul to the inferno would have no effect. Armed with two buckets she made several trips between the trough and the burning barn, but heat and smoke soon defeated her and she sank to her knees. Knelt there for a long while, until the flames consumed the freshly peeled logs, leaving only a smoking pile.

Green timbers wouldn't burn that fast without help, and in a puff of breeze she detected the pungent odor of coal oil. The rider had made sure this one wouldn't be put out.

With a sigh that made her smoke-burned lungs ache, she rose, retrieved the Winchester from beside the water trough, and called for Belle. After unsaddling the mare and turning her into the corral with the others who continued to trot circles and squeal nervously, she trudged to the one-room cabin. Once inside she found the hollow silence unbearable. Loneliness crept its way into her heart and soul, and that in itself was bad enough without the added burden of fury over the deliberate fire.

And so the colonel's war had begun in earnest. Now that winter was over, the roundup done, all the innuendoes and veiled threats spouted by Dunkirk's men would come to pass. In the end he would probably win and get her land, no matter how hard she fought.

After she washed her hands and face, she tugged off the dusty boots and skinned out of her clothes. Every muscle ached, none so much as her heart. What should she do? Despairing of an answer she crawled into bed. Lying in the dark, she thought of the ranch in Texas. The bright and airy rooms in the sprawling adobe house. The young Mexican woman who scrubbed the pine board floors till they gleamed, aired the blankets on the porch railings, and cooked delicious meals that filled the rooms with their savory aromas. How she missed it.

Damn that Dunkirk!

He'd sent one of his rowdies to burn down her barn even before the hands could finish building it He wasn't satisfied with stealing all the government land for his own, he had to have what belonged to all the honest decent folk too. Probably would have burned the whole place if she hadn't rode in when she had. Damn him to hell, how could she fight him?

She thought of Mitchell Fallon and his words of hate. A brutal man who would shoot anybody who tried to fight back. Could he have been the one who torched the barn? He'd left early enough to reach the ranch ahead of her. Barn burning didn't seem the kind of thing a man like him would do. He was here for much more specialized work than burning barns with that Colt strapped low on his hip and those killer's eyes hard as stone and devoid of emotion. But if he had set the fire, she hoped the bullet she'd put in him festered and gave him gangrene.

After lying in bed for what seemed like hours, she finally gave up. Standing naked in the center of the dark room she shivered and hugged herself. Spring nights were chilly and goose bumps rose up her arms and flitted down across her bare breasts.

She felt her way across the room and started a fire in the cook stove. Once the flames crackled she filled the kettle. A hot bath would help her sleep, and the business of preparing one would keep her thoughts on something besides her troubles.

While the water heated she lit a lamp and, wrapping herself in a quilt, sat cross-legged on the floor. From under the bed she pulled out a small humpbacked chest, opened it, and removed a music box and several metal disks. Winding the crank and inserting a disk, she shed the rough cowhand exterior as easily as she'd removed the Kentucky jeans, flannel shirt and union suit.

The lovely strains of Chopin soothed her soul, and dancing so unencumbered freed her from the rigid restraints of her singular life. She began to dance, bending and turning like a lithe willow in a gentle breeze. She ended the dance by sinking to the floor on the heaped quilt as the melody faded. The utter silence that followed was broken only by her breathing and the muted thumping of her heart.

Far off in the distance she heard the echoing forlorn howl of a wolf and an almost indistinct reply from another of its kind. With a shudder she rose, poured the hissing water into the wash pan, and soaped up a cloth. Eyes closed she began to rub the soft fabric slowly over her bare flesh. Under one arm, along the swell of her breast to the nipple that hardened under the touch.

An image assaulted her. Mitchell Fallon's green eyes sparking fire while he preened like a savage animal. The man continued to bedevil her and she wanted rid of him, in the flesh and in her mind. Shivering, she slipped into a flannel nightgown and extinguished the lamp.

He went to bed with her, no matter how she tried to shut him out, and she curled beneath the quilt, pulling her knees up under her chin. He could come in the night to attack her, or to trail his sensual lips and long fingers over places that might awaken the feelings the tough side of Charlie Houston did not acknowledge.

Mitch Fallon sat astride the skittish black stallion and gazed down at the smoking ruin amid the few poor structures of the Double H Ranch.

Foolish, stupid woman. How could she possibly think she could win this battle, and why would she want to? Even if she was a man all the odds were stacked against her. Why didn't she go back where she came from and marry up with somebody, settle down and raise some young'uns and make bread and grow a garden? Why didn't she leave before she got hurt? Before she got *killed?*

He swallowed harshly, thickly. Dammit, he hadn't expected this. The enemy was supposed to be out there. Someone he could kill so he'd feel better. Not some woman. Not someone who made him remember....

The memories overpowered him. Celia and their firstborn, a lovely little girl as pretty as her copper-skinned mother. He had called the child Fawn because of her doelike eyes, but Celia had insisted on a white child's name because she herself had one, even though she was a full-blooded Sioux. He could not even think about his family without becoming enraged. Everywhere he went he looked for the men who had killed his wife and child.

Annoyed at the unexpected lapse into the past, Mitch

lifted the reins to turn the big stallion and ride back to Dunkirk's spread. A light went on in the cabin, a feeble glow that brightened the windows and made him hesitate. He wasn't sure why he didn't just ride away, yet he paused a moment longer when a graceful shadow swayed across the lighted square and disappeared from sight.

What the hell? Someone was dancing in there. Whirling and twisting, bending and swaying.

He leaned forward in the saddle, felt the thickness of his manhood, a throbbing heat he'd thought long dead. Drained away from him like Celia's blood in the dusty street of Bismarck.

The stallion shifted angrily, wanting to go, held in place only because the man on his back was his master, with a will stronger and darker than he himself.

Raising to stand in the stirrups, he lifted throbbing loins from the caress of the leather. In the cabin below lamplight outlined the lean, feminine body. The woman raised her arms, turned to reveal a contour of lush breasts; a firm leg lifted so he could imagine he looked into her innermost secret places.

Good God, what was wrong with him? Sitting up here like a peeping Tom, some adolescent youth getting stirred up over forbidden sights. Yet he couldn't move away as the figure twirled and bent and disappeared once again from the window.

In the distance wolves howled, the stallion sawed at his bit and moaned, a gentle breeze picked up to cool the sweat of Fallon's ardor. Still he watched, a man filled with hate enraptured by an unexpected glimpse of pure beauty. A beauty that exacted no penalty from him for his enjoyment.

Soon enough he would go back to the world in which he chose to live, and that too made him very angry.

Hell, if he hadn't been thinking of Celia and Fawn, hadn't been treading dangerously close to reliving what he could never,

never recapture, he wouldn't have been aroused by the magical vision down there in the first place. The unreal occurrence reached inside him and ripped at his tortured soul until he wanted to shout with anguish. He never expected to see such a thing out here on the Montana plains where life was reduced to a harsh day-to-day struggle for survival It had taken him by surprise, that was all.

How he felt meant nothing in the scheme of things. He had no intention of ever experiencing again the intensified emotion that loving a beautiful woman inspired.

Yanking the stallion's head around he whipped the reins and spurred the taut flanks. He rode as fast and hard as he could away from the sight of the cabin and the images that painfully exposed the futility of his own existence.

Three

By dawn the Double H hands had returned from Miles City, a bit chagrined when they caught sight of the smoking rubble that had once been a barn.

Ritter clattered up onto the porch and tapped meekly on the door. Miss Houston was mad at him before, and now she would probably jerk his shoulders up around his ears. He figured somehow him not being here for the fire would turn out to be his fault, as if he ought to have known it would happen.

Already dressed in jeans and a flannel shirt, but still in her stocking feet, Charlie swung open the door and gazed up at him. Her eyes were so black the pupils didn't show, her skin the color of coffee with a healthy dash of thick cream added. She was the prettiest woman Ritter had ever seen, tough and sturdily built but at the same time delicately turned so that every movement was feminine.

He gestured over his shoulder at the smoldering mass of ashes. "How'd it happen?"

"That no-account Dunkirk must've sent one of his men to set it. Did a good job too." She shrugged, looked down at her small stocking feet. "Didn't even get it plumb built. Reckon that'll put some of you boys to work."

Belatedly Ritter jerked his hat from his head. He hated

what else he had to tell her on top of the fire, hated it so much that he just forgot and spilled out that name she'd asked him never to use. He just kept doing it like he was dumb or something. *Ma'am, ma'am, ma'am.* It seemed all he was able to blurt out when he was around her. And here it was, rolling off his tongue again. He screwed up his face and shifted from one foot to the other. By the look she gave him he knew it was too late to try to take it back.

Though she'd said it before at least a hundred times, she repeated with quiet exasperation, "Call me Houston, Ritter. I've told you I don't cotton to ma'am much."

He nodded, uncomfortable more with his piece of news than with the expected request. "Yes'm. I mean… *okay*, fine. Chocco ain't comin' back, ma'am, I mean *Houston*." He let his voice trail away on the last syllable. How dumb he felt calling her that. It would never do.

The news about their cook jolted her. "Chocco? Why not? What happened?"

"Well, he said… he told me to say he liked riding the trail fine, doing the cooking and taking care of the chuck wagon… but well, he said when it comes to ranching, he just ain't cut out for it. Said he's heading back down to the Brazos, hopes to latch on to a herd he can cook for."

The surly Chocco had said little after Matt was killed, even though he had stayed on for the winter. For that she was grateful, but his leaving sure did put her in a bind.

"Any of the other boys cook?" she asked after thinking on it awhile.

He had already backed all the way to the edge of the porch just in case she got physical, and he began to shake his head. "I don't reckon they can, ma'am. Uh—"

"Never mind, Ritter. Thank you for telling me. I'll get my

boots on and... well, hell, I don't know what. Chocco left the chuck wagon?"

He flinched and raised his shoulders in reply. He wasn't used to a woman who used words like hell and dammit. It wasn't natural somehow. He hadn't paid attention to much of anything in Miles City but finding him a pretty girl and knocking back some beers, and so couldn't remember exactly everything the old cook had to say before he took off.

When it came to grub, all Ritter knew was spooning beans off his plate. Every cowboy could boil coffee. That wasn't saying much about what it would taste like, plus that didn't have anything to do with cooking anyway. One thing he knew for dang sure, and it worried him a heap more than the missing cook. If those gunslingers of Dunkirk's drew down on him, he'd probably get himself killed because he didn't know anything about one of those fancy side arms much less how to shoot at someone.

"Tell the men I'll be on down, we'll figure something out." Charlie shut the door before Ritter could reply.

She leaned her forehead up against the cool wood for a moment, then went to get her boots on. Sometimes you reached a point where things could only get better, and she figured she wasn't too far off that mark.

The chuck wagon was parked out back of the bunkhouse, tongue pointed toward Texas, as if the surly old cook had left a final message. On the trail he would have put the tongue toward the North Star each night so the drovers would know the direction in which they should travel the next day. This, though, was a sign of where Chocco had gone, and maybe a hint that she too would do well to go back where she belonged.

Shrugging, she began an immediate search of the contents of the wagon. She lifted the cover from a bowl stuck away in the grub box and took a whiff.

"It's sourdough starter, I know that much," she said aloud. "At least we'll have biscuits."

She puttered around in there quite a spell while the hungry hands moaned and milled about like cattle. She rattled spoons and unwrapped supplies until it finally occurred to her that they would need a cook fire. She put two of the boys to building one.

Belatedly she realized it would be easier to cook breakfast on her cookstove in the cabin, if anything about cooking could be easy. Since she was already committed, though, she stuck to her guns, digging her way through the unfamiliar utensils until she finally located the Dutch oven. Heartened by the find, she dipped flour into an empty bowl and then spooned in some of the gooey sourdough starter.

Ritter watched anxiously. He'd never before seen a woman who couldn't cook, except maybe a soiled dove or two, and of course they'd never had to cook 'cause what they gave their men had nothing to do with a cook stove or satisfying an empty belly. This woman, his boss, who insisted he call her Houston, rolled her shirtsleeves up to her elbows and with a terrible expression on her face stuck both hands right down into that mess she'd made. After a while she lifted them out, long strands of dough hanging from each finger like drool from a suckling calf.

"Pour me out some more flour, Ritter, would you?"

He obeyed but felt foolish, looked around to make sure none of the boys saw him doing such a sissy job. There was a limit to what even a jingler would do.

She finally had this great big wad of rubbery stuff that she played around in for a while longer, then started making balls and tucking them into the Dutch oven. When she had it layered up pretty good, she covered the thing and nestled it down in one side of the blazing fire.

He couldn't keep his mouth shut any longer. "Ma'am, I

think you're supposed to put coals on top and sorta heap 'em up around that thing."

She was so dithered she didn't even make anything of him calling her the forbidden ma'am, instead pursed her mouth into a pretty pout that made Ritter wonder why some man hadn't grabbed her up a long time ago.

"Well, yes, of course. I know that," she told him. "You do it, Ritter, I'm looking for something else to cook."

He obeyed. He figured he'd probably do anything she asked him to, bar none.

Eventually she found a slab of salt-cured fatback wrapped in a greasy cloth, sliced some off, and tossed the pieces in a long-handled black fry pan. That too she placed on the fire, jiggling the burning wood around until she made a level place. Flames licked up around the sides of the pan and meat began to sizzle right away, then caught fire. Enormous orange flames, fed by the grease, leaped from the skillet.

"Ritter, dammit, give me a hand here," she yelled.

She smelled hair burning and staggered back away from the fire before her head could go up in flames.

He scooped up a double handful of dirt and threw it over the burning meat.

She stood there a moment staring down at the mess, grease and curls of black meat poking up out of the brown earth, then tramped to where the hands were gathered, a safe distance from her and the cook fire.

Blowing singed hair from her sweating face, she addressed the amazed men. "At least the biscuits are cooking. I'm sorry about the meat. If one of you ever says a word about this ever to anyone, I'll send you riding, you understand?"

They all nodded somberly, but she could tell they were just about to bust out laughing.

"That's all right, ma'am," one of the men ventured, and someone chuckled.

"Don't call me that," she shouted.

"Sir, then," came a low voice.

She whirled to see Ritter, thumbs hanging from his pockets and an amused, innocent expression on his boyish face.

"I can make coffee, I know how to do that," he offered quickly before she could come down on him for something. He skittered off to do so, seeing this whole thing escalating into a disaster that might cause all the hands to quit This woman rode like a man and worked like a man, who could expect her to cook, anyway?

He filled the mammoth pot with water, threw in several hands of Arbuckle coffee, and turned to set it on the fire just as the lid to the Dutch oven lifted with an ominous hiss. He watched fascinated, while swelling sourdough biscuits pushed the heavy lid off into the fire. Then a mushrooming white mass oozed out over the sides of the iron pot. In the hope that what was left in there might accidentally cook into something the boys could eat, he just backed off and let 'er rip.

Charlie scooted for the house, muttering under her breath about men who were so helpless they'd starve before they'd cook a meal. Safely hidden inside she opened a can of peaches and sat down at the table to spoon the luscious golden halves from their thick syrup and onto her tongue that felt like it was coated with smoke.

She would most definitely have to ride into Miles City and see if she could hire a cook, or every man on the place would desert the Double H before she even got the ranch producing.

"I won't fail you, I won't," she said aloud. She'd made the promise to the memory of her father uncounted times during the long winter months. While alone in the cabin night after night, all she'd had to think about were her memories and the raw grief. But it was time she started to live in the present and face her responsibilities.

She would make a go of this place one way or another, and damn anyone who tried to stop her.

Mitch refused the fat cigar Dunkirk offered as well as the leather chair he indicated. Lazed near the wide windows he studied the portly uniformed man who had hired him to do his dirty work. Dunkirk was a bastard, that was for sure, but he had the upper hand in this territory because he knew what it took to win. As for Mitch, he didn't much care. Win or lose was all the same to him.

"We're going to finish up this business this summer," the colonel railed. "I'm tired of these cowboys riding up from Texas after we did all the hard work here in Montana and expecting to cut their slice from our pie. This land is mine, all of it. I broke trail when no one else had the guts. I wintered and froze my ass and figured out how to get enough land to do me any good when the damned government wanted to parcel it out to every lazy sodbuster and soldier who come along. Men who don't know anything but to hold out their hand.

"By God I'll not see it torn down by these three-up outfits who'll steal the water even though they haven't got enough head to hold a decent barbecue, or a bunch of nesters who'll plow up the grass and butcher my cows to feed their snot-nosed kids."

The colonel let his gaze wander around the room, taking in the half-dozen fighting men he'd gathered there. "I want the water choked off first, and you can start with the Rocking R and the Double H. They're watering on the Porcupine where it makes that great big loop onto their land 'fore it comes back on mine. Come a dry spell they'll use it up. I want it stopped."

His close-set eyes came to rest on Fallon. "You got anything against going after a woman?"

"Woman... man. Makes no difference to me," Mitch said.

"You keep an eye on that Houston girlie. She's no ordinary woman, and she can shoot too. I don't aim to see any of my hands gunned down, and especially not by any female, you got that? If you don't think you can handle that, say so now. I got men who won't think twice, but I'm spread thin here. They're closing in on me from all sides, and on top of that, the savages are pilfering horses and cattle every chance they get. I gotta put guards on my herds, for God's sake.

"Hell, it ain't bad enough the government throws all kinds of barriers in the way, they don't even have the gumption to take care of this Indian problem out here, once and for all. What they need to do is bring in enough soldiers to wipe out the bloody savages, make room for us white men."

Mitch turned from the fiery stare in the colonel's little pig eyes. He ought to just ride out. What was he doing here working for this filth, anyway? It was probably the most low-down job a man could have. Still, it didn't much matter what he did anymore, did it? Dying one way was as good as dying another.

The colonel continued to watch him while rolling his cigar around between his lips until he had the end wetted. "I can't spare anyone from ranch chores for a few days. All these other ranchers hiring leaves me shorthanded. I've sent for some more men, but in the meantime I want you to get to know the enemy, Fallon, nose around."

❁

Radine Granville was a professional, and she plied the oldest profession very well. She didn't mind tending bar once in a while, and would do so with good nature because she liked Lance Brannigan O'Shea, owner of the Powder Keg. But they had a deal. If a man came in wanting a poke, she left the bar and did her pleasuring.

She was proud to say that no man had led her down the path to sinning, nor had poverty been to blame. She just plain liked sex and she liked to please men. She couldn't imagine anything better than getting paid for something she enjoyed doing so much.

This particular night had turned out to be quiet. The few drifters who dropped in didn't want much of anything but a mug of beer and to be left alone. Most of the good men were working on the surrounding ranches, coming in so beat at the end of a long day that all they could manage was to fall into their bunks. Come Saturday night they'd all come to town to howl and things would be different. So Radine mopped at the bar top and refilled an occasional mug while Lance did some whiskey inventory and got his next order ready in the back room.

She glanced up at the sound of the batwing doors swishing open. The gunslinger who worked for Colonel Dunkirk came in, like some kind of sleek cat on the prowl. Radine eyed him warily. She liked most men, dirty or clean, as long as they treated her right. Meanness she couldn't stand, wouldn't put up with, and Lance always backed her up on that.

This one wore a gun on his right hip, but that didn't scare her nearly as much as his eyes. Though he'd been in more than once, she still hadn't taken his full measure. He was one hell of a man, that she could tell in a glance.

He ambled to the bar, checking out the few patrons with more than casual curiosity. When he finally stood before her,

Radine swept her gaze slowly and deliberately from the top of
the bar right on up to the brim of the black Stetson. She'd never
met a man yet who could keep his true intent from showing in
his eyes, and despite her earlier assessment, wished his weren't
now in shadow. Then he shifted just a bit and the glow from the
wall lamps illuminated the emerald-green depths of those eyes.
For a brief instant she caught a glimpse of a deep melancholy
reflected there, and she yearned to reach out and soothe him.
Before she could he shut down the vision, as if he'd realized
she'd seen into his soul he slammed the door.

Nonplussed, she continued her inspection of the rugged
features, stopping at the scar. A slash through his left eyebrow
looked like a jag of wicked lightning that had spawned a great
white streak in his black hair.

She shivered and turned away. "What'll you have?" she
asked, and was surprised that her voice trembled.

"A beer... first." His tone showed he wasn't well pleased with
her once-over.

She drew a draft, set it before him, and stared at the foam
that dribbled down one side of the glass. "And second?" she
asked, amazed that for the first time in her career a man had
caused her to go nearly speechless.

He shot her a piercing look so cold that she dropped a
glass she had absentmindedly begun to polish. It hit the floor
with a sharp explosion, but she didn't flinch, even when a few
splinters nicked at her ankle like insect bites. This man she
couldn't read and that worried her. Desire and fear stirred
together in the pit of her stomach. At first she thought there
wouldn't be enough money in the world to put her in a room
alone with him, yet in the next moment she wanted to give
herself to him for nothing.

He finished the beer without telling her what he wanted

second, never once glancing at the bare swell of her creamy breasts. Nor did he seem to notice she'd broken a glass to smithereens.

"And second," she prodded, afraid of his reply. If he wanted her, would she take him upstairs?

Mitch found he had been staring with fierce concentration in the mirror above the whore's head, and it was making her mighty nervous. He shrugged. "I've changed my mind."

Vaguely disappointed that his second wish wasn't for her, Radine considered coming back with a snappy remark, but held her tongue. It wouldn't be wise to rankle this one, and she had decided she didn't want to be in a room alone with him anyway.

Fallon thought she wasn't bad-looking, kind of like a plump, ripe strawberry, with red hair and flushed skin dusted with freckles, her cheeks brightly painted as were her lips. She'd be mighty sweet in bed, even though she was a bit older than most doves he'd run across. He even considered smothering his growing fire with this little redheaded whore, but changed his mind in the instant it took him to remember what had fanned that fire in the first place. Charlie Houston would not be easily forgotten by going to bed with a whore. Besides his feelings went deeper than that, and once again he wondered why. There would never be a meeting ground for the two of them, even if he did decide to pursue her. Besides, she was just a tough cowpoke who happened to be female. Probably had no use for men, and certainly not for the likes of him.

After he left Radine realized that she hadn't asked his name. He would make an interesting but dangerous lover. She even felt sorry for the man, for she'd seen his like before and he would probably come to no good.

Provoked by her own frustration, she ran off the remaining three customers and pulled the heavy wooden shutters over the swinging doors of the saloon. She stood there with her back up against the rough wood for several minutes, waiting for the storm of emotions to quiet so she could get to sleep without being bothered by itches she couldn't scratch.

Four

The morning after the barn burned Charlie set two of the men to rebuilding it and rode out for Miles City to talk to the sheriff. For a good long while she could hear the distant rhythmic chuck of axes from the wooded slope. Yancey had promised to keep a guard on the place to prevent a recurrence of what had happened the night before. Maybe what she really needed was a gun hand like Mitchell Fallon. Her men were cowboys used to punching cattle, and while they might pick off a rattler or a coyote with a rifle, none were used to shooting men.

During the three-hour ride she had plenty of time to think. It disturbed her that the dark brooding visage of Mitchell Fallon continued to disrupt her plans for protecting the ranch and hiring a cook. Why he should haunt her was a mystery. She hadn't thought seriously of men since her crush on Yancey Barton when he thought her merely a child. And she certainly had no business considering for one moment even a passing interest in a hired gunslinger. Especially not one who worked for the other side in this battle for range land. If she were serious about anyone, it should be Cal Malone. He treated her like a friend, but had made it clear more than once that they might team up. Charlie sensed, though, that he was more interested in combining the two ranches than in a romantic pairing.

He couldn't quite get over the loss of his wife Becky. Such a joining would be practical since the two shared a north to south boundary line and butted up against the southwest corner of the colonel's Circle D. But that's all it would be. A marriage minus passion wasn't desirable.

The rumble of approaching hoof beats brought Charlie out of her reverie, and she reined in quickly. Three Indian braves rode up on her from a wooded gully. She recognized Gray Horse and his son Spotted Moon, both Northern Cheyenne, but the third brave was a stranger to her.

Last fall, she and her herd had no sooner arrived on the Double H than Gray Horse had shown up. Even before they had started work on the bunkhouse, the first of two structures they'd built before winter set in, the Indian had been there, explaining in his elusive way that the two peoples shared this land. She had promptly presented him with a longhorn steer for his tribe to butcher, and Gray Horse had reciprocated by giving her a fine tanned deerskin. Even so, friendship between the white man and Indian on the Montana plains was a touchy situation.

Charlie considered the present danger, and in spite of a thundering heart greeted the three ominous braves.

Spotted Moon leaped gracefully from his small paint, while Gray Horse and the other brave remained mounted.

"Split Skirt," Spotted Moon said. "I am pleased that winter did not chill your heart."

Charlie remained in the saddle. Spotted Moon was a huge Indian, and she felt more secure looking down on him. She smiled at the name the Cheyenne had given her. "And you wintered well too, I see."

He gazed off into the distance beyond her shoulder. "Old Fox passed into the land of the gods."

She suppressed a shudder. Old Fox was the medicine man,

so dried and feeble he had seemed to be at least two hundred years old, though of course she knew he wasn't. Last fall, a week or so after she presented Gray Horse with the steer, he and Spotted Moon had carried the old man to her cabin on a travois. He proceeded to conduct some kind of a ritual over her and her home. Gray Horse and Spotted Moon had not explained the ceremony, but they beamed as if Old Fox was doing her an extreme honor. She behaved as if she understood the ceremony and smiled a lot, feeling rather foolish.

Later she had repaid the visit, riding up on the small family band of Northern Cheyenne in their encampment near the Elk River. She and Spotted Moon's wife, who spoke no English, had discovered a kinship that Charlie couldn't explain. She held the woman's child in her arms, cupped a hand over the downy hair, and closed her eyes in odd contentment when the baby nuzzled her breast. The enormous swell of emotion that charged through her at that moment had remained with Charlie during the long winter. She often thought of the band out there in their tepees in the freezing cold. The tiny beautiful child sewn in thick skins to keep away the ravages of the brutal north wind.

Remembering that incident, she gazed down at Spotted Moon from the back of her horse. "And your wife and child, how are they?"

"Our women and children are hungry," Spotted Moon said, pride tinged with an undertone of resentment. "The buffalo are few and the iron rails will soon run them all from our land. If we do not fight soon we will have nothing left. We would not wish to fight Split Skirt. Old Fox paid you much honor, and your cattle have multiplied grazing our land."

Charlie suppressed a smile of admiration. There were still plenty of buffalo on the vast plains, but Spotted Moon certainly understood diplomacy. "You would honor me if you rode to my ranch and told my foreman that you are to have two steers."

Before Spotted Moon could react, Gray Horse spat something quickly and gestured with the feathered lance he carried. Everyone looked at once including Charlie. Atop a rise with the vast Montana sky at his back sat a lone rider on an enormous black horse. He appeared to pay no attention to their sudden interest in him, but the third brave sent out a spine-tingling cry that made Charlie's skin crawl.

Spotted Moon gestured, obviously anxious to ride away.

Gray Horse spoke again.

"My father says we must come to the ranch when you will be there. He says we want three beeves, and that we could take the cattle we wish at any time, but we will not." The brave glanced once more toward the rise where the rider had been, and so did she. The man was gone, leaving behind a fine trail of dust that rose from beyond an outcropping of red boulders.

Before she could turn back and reply, the three Indians rode away, the stranger letting loose with another of his shrill cries. She was a little more than uneasy at the encounter, for it hadn't escaped her notice that all three of the braves were painted as if for battle.

That wasn't all that worried Charlie as she headed once again for Miles City. What was Mitch Fallon doing spying on her and what was he up to? She certainly had plenty to speak to the sheriff about when she got to town.

Sheriff Clarence Newton, referred to behind his back as Sheriff Newt, frowned at her when she clattered into his office and slammed the door. She'd worked up a full head of steam just thinking about Dunkirk and his crooked ways.

"Purty day, ain't it?" the laconic sheriff said without rising.

"If it weren't for the smoke coming off that heap of rubble that used to be my barn, it might be."

The sheriff raised gray eyebrows, the only hair for quite a stretch up his forehead. "Someone kick over a lantern?"

Charlie gritted her teeth and slipped off her leather gloves, folding them over one hand to have something to do until her voice would work right. When it did her reply ricocheted around the small office.

"You know damn well they didn't. Some no-account poured coal oil all over the place and lit it afire."

"How do you know that?" he asked, and squinted up at her.

"I could smell it, and I saw him ride out."

"Last night? Who was it?" Sheriff Newt finally showed some concern, but no doubt for the wrong reasons.

She couldn't really blame him too much for his lethargy. Colonel Dunkirk pretty well ran the district and he intended to see things went his way. If Newton didn't cooperate, well, he'd just be run out of town or shot some dark night. Newton knew full well that the colonel wanted her and all the small ranchers gone, and would do just about anything to accomplish that goal.

"I suppose I could wire the territorial marshal, let him come on down and investigate," she said in a tight voice.

"No need in that, little lady. I'll look right into it. Said you saw him? Who was this feller?"

"It was dark. He wasn't real big and he rode a gray, maybe an Appaloosa. I took some shots at him. Could be I hit him."

"Not unless he decided to bleed somewhere besides at the doc's you didn't. No one come in shot up that I know of." Newton rose and took a new Kalispell Stetson off the hat rack. "Not much to go on, but I'll check around. Anything else?"

Charlie slapped the gloves smartly in the palm of her hand. She was as tall as the graying sheriff and took advantage of that fact by glowering right into his eyes. "He comes back, I won't miss. You might pass that around while you're checking," she snapped, and jerked the door open to stalk from his office.

Out on the boardwalk she swiveled on one boot heel and jigged down two steps where she bumped smack into the broad chest of Mitchell Fallon as he emerged from the alley. He grunted and automatically caught at her, his large hands closing around her upper arms.

His remarkable eyes flared for just an instant, then he said in that mocking voice, "Pardon me, ma'am."

"You shut up," she said loudly, and shoved out of his grasp. "Stop following me around and stay off my place too, or I just might shoot you as well."

Mitch batted his eyes and watched Charlie stride off down the street toward the saloon. He waited until the doors stopped their wild swinging at her back before moving.

"Woman must drink panther piss for breakfast," he remarked aloud to himself. At the hitching post he unwound the reins of his waiting horse and as he rode past the saloon, tipped his hat solemnly. Whoever she was looking to light into next deserved sympathy as well. He couldn't blame the lady considering the tight hole she'd dug for herself. She was apt to be a lot more put out before Dunkirk was through with her. He wished he could just go tell her to go back home where she belonged and be done with it. Probably wouldn't do much good, though. She appeared just ornery enough to put up a good fight, and that was too bad. It would no doubt get her killed.

Charlie's heart thudded at her temples for a full five minutes after she sat down alone at a table inside the half-empty saloon. Her arms throbbed where he had held them and she couldn't get those frosty eyes out of her mind. She glanced around the murky room. It was too early in the day for much more than ne'er-do-wells and the usual three or four poker players in the dark little place. Still, she could leave word here that she was on the lookout for a good cook. She grinned wryly. Perhaps she'd modify that and just say she was looking for any kind of cook. Forget the good part.

Radine came strolling in from the back room, eyes still swollen with sleep, and Charlie hailed her. She liked Radine because she was honest and didn't care a whit what anyone thought. Though there were other doves in Miles City, she was extremely popular. Charlie could only guess why. The woman was a bit too plump and some older than the other girls, yet the men sought her out. Charlie had often overheard them talking about "good old Radine," and how she could fix up a sore body.

Radine fingered at her mussed red hair and laughed merrily as she sat down with Charlie.

"Early day, isn't it?" Her big eyes, bright as dew-touched sloe berries, studied Charlie's somber expression.

"Looking for a cook," Charlie told her. "Thought maybe Lance would pass the word, and you too."

Radine nodded. "Wouldn't hurt if you stuck up a notice over by the bar too." She fingered the ribbon at her throat, glanced up at Charlie. "You see that new guy the colonel hired?"

"He wouldn't make a good cook."

"Well, I wouldn't mind him doing some cooking with me, hon." Radine giggled like a girl, a habit Charlie found most disconcerting in this woman more than a dozen years her senior.

"Well, Fallon scares me, and he ought to you too," Charlie told Radine, remembering the man's cold regard. "Men like that don't care who they hurt."

"Fallon? Is that his name?" Radine rubbed up and down her arms with both hands as if suddenly chilled. "Maybe you're right. I've pleasured more than a few who thought nothing of belting me around afterward. What happened to your cook?"

"Went back to Texas, and if I had any sense that's what I'd do, too."

"Aw, you don't want to leave this wonderful place." Radine gestured around the primitive saloon, the whiskey barrels holding up raw board planks that served as a bar, the crude tables and chairs, the boarded-up window holes that would soon be uncovered for the short, hot summer.

The two women laughed.

"You'll tell Lance then?" Charlie said and stood to leave.

"About needing a cook, yeah." Radine traced through a crack on the table with a chipped nail. "Charlie... if I... would you... I mean, could I come to call sometime?"

The question stopped Charlie in her tracks and she turned to regard the sincere, round-cheeked face, untouched by paint this early in the day. Radine was just about the only woman in town willing to be seen talking to her without glancing around nervously to see who was watching. She was surprised to see the eagerness in the woman's expression.

"Why, I think I'd like that a lot. Please do come out sometime. And the next time I'm in town, maybe we could meet somewhere...well, maybe somewhere for lunch, or something."

Radine beamed. "That would be wonderful."

Charlie took her leave, repeating her invitation once again. She didn't want Radine to think she wasn't sincere.

After leaving the Powder Keg she posted a "Cook Wanted" notice at every business in town, and spoke to several townspeople about her need, but came away empty handed. What hands had been laid off after spring roundup had either ridden on or couldn't cook. She was surprised to learn that Dunkirk had hired a lot of those let go by the smaller ranchers. He must be building an army out there at the Circle D.

At the mercantile she studied several samples of barbed wire thoughtfully, stopped a moment to touch a finger to the two-strand Gliddens. How wicked it looked.

"Montana lands are no place for that devil's creation," a voice at her back said. "Man rides into it on a horse it rips his guts out. Him nor his beast can get untangled. He'll die thrashing around there on the ground."

She shuddered at Colonel Dunkirk's implication, catching an underlying threat that had nothing to do with his sorry remark about barbed wire. Before she could bring herself to reply, he'd changed his tone.

"I'd say we all did right well at roundup, wouldn't you, little lady?"

"Don't call me *little lady* and I won't call you little *man*," she said back at him.

Dunkirk chortled and patted his amble girth. "Well, now, ma'am, I don't hardly think it would be fitting to call me little man, not by any stretch of the imagination." He dropped his glance so that it stopped deliberately at the level of her breasts. Though bound under the loose flannel shirt, her nipples hardened in defense of his visual insinuation.

"You are no gentlemen, sir," she said.

"And neither are you, my dear," Dunkirk replied. "And you would do well to stop acting like one before I forget that."

The threat was there, unspoken and terrifying. He would give her no quarter despite her being a member of the gentler sex.

"One of your men rides onto my land again, no matter his intent, and I will shoot him."

"Ah, my dear, you do that and I will see you hanged."

"You'll play the devil, sir." She whirled and walked away, a mixture of fear and raw fury churning within her until her throat burned with it.

She headed back to the Double H without having solved any

of her problems, the most urgent of which at the moment was someone to cook for the hands. All she had really succeeded in doing was to further alienate everyone she came in contact with.

Soon after she turned her horse into the corral at the ranch Yancey Barton rode in with news that two of the hands had lit out, saying they wouldn't work hard all day and then have only soggy biscuits for supper, not even for Matt Houston's daughter.

"Besides," he confided, "I think they went to work for Dunkirk. He's been nosing around trying to hire up all the men who work for the small spreads. Figures that's as good a way as any to drive us out."

"I heard that in town. And you, Yancey, what about you?" she asked.

"Me? I'd as soon shoot the son of a bitch as talk to him, but I know better."

"No, I mean, how much longer will it be before you ride out too? Forget Dunkirk."

"Miss Charlie, your daddy hired me on when I was green as a pile of fresh manure, and he put me to handling the worst chores around the ranch. Cutting wood for the kitchen, swamping out the barns, milking the dad-blamed cows, and I never quit on him. Not once did I even think of it, and me just a kid who didn't even have good sense. So what makes you think a little thing like exploding biscuits and burning barns is going to drive me off?"

The man's crinkly blue eyes twinkled as he fiddled with the latigo on his saddle, unbuckling the strap with hands as tough as the leather he stroked.

Despite the lump in her throat she grinned at this sturdy cowboy who had held her in his arms while Matt Houston was put under the ground, and patted her back and told her, "Go ahead and cry, little sweetheart." He'd been around the ranch as long as she could remember and when she was fifteen and he twenty-five she'd fallen in love with him. That had matured now into the love she knew she would have felt for an older brother or perhaps a beloved uncle.

She pulled herself from the reverie, said thoughtfully, "I ran across Spotted Moon and Gray Horse wanting some more steers, and that gunslinger was dogging my tracks plain as can be. Then to make matters worse I met up with Dunkirk in town and he all but threatened me if I don't sell out to him. As if that weren't enough, the sheriff just plain said he doesn't intend to do anything about the barn burning.

"It's been a hell of a day. Makes me wish I... oh, dammit, Yancey, how can I give up Matt's dream?"

He studied her for a long moment, moving his hat round and round in work-roughened fingers. Then he said, "Don't you have any dreams of your own, sweetheart? Maybe it's time you thought of yourself. Matt Houston always did just what he wanted to do, don't you think he'd want his daughter to do the same?"

Grimly she bit her lips together. "I am doing what I want to do. I love this ranch, every bit as much as he did, and I won't let some sidewinding son of a —"

"Whoa, Miss Charlie," Yancey said. "No need in taking a cussin' fit. I didn't intend to rile you. Let me speak to the men, we'll rustle up some grub like we would were we on the trail by our own selves for a few days till you can get someone out to do the cooking. One thing at a time is what I always say. Maybe we can keep 'em from riding if they know you're trying."

He stopped twisting the hat and looked right at her. "Them Cheyenne show up, you want me to cut out a couple of head?"

"Yes, I do. I can't see letting their women and kids starve, though I don't expect it'll be much longer before they're driven right out of this country. I don't know what they'll do, Yancey, I surely don't, but I can't help them any more than that. I'm afraid no one can. It's like they're destined to disappear from the face of the earth to make way for the white man. Doesn't seem fair when you think about it, does it?"

"They're just red savages, Miss Charlie, don't fret about them so. They'll make out. Hell, they been killing each other for hundreds of years. What you gotta do is keep peace with them, like the rest of the ranchers. And you're right, soon enough they'll all be gone. This land is too precious to be left to a bunch of wild Indians who don't know what it's truly good for."

Tears filled her eyes, thinking of the women and children in the Cheyenne camp. The babe she'd held in her arms would be walking soon, and chattering and laughing. What had he ever done to deserve such a fate, or any of them, for that matter? But Yancey was right, there was only so much she could do.

"See they get four steers. And see if there's a cow that's fresh without a calf. I'm sure those babies could use some milk. If we can't spare that many, then we'll soon go under anyway."

He palmed his hat down on his head and nodded. "One thing's for certain, Miss Charlie, you're for sure your daddy's daughter, and I can't fault you for that."

The next morning at dawn Charlie saddled up and rode out to the southwestern section of the ranch. After roundup and branding were finished they had turned a large portion of the herd into the rich grassland there. It was fed by a meandering loop of Porcupine Creek that left the Circle D to water both her land and Cal's for several miles before flowing back onto the colonel's spread. She wanted to see for herself how the spring calves were faring.

And that's where she rode right up on Fallon. She thought later that it was almost as if their meeting was meant, and there wasn't anything either of them could do about it. The country was so big, the trails so remote from one another it shouldn't have happened, but it did.

As she rode she sang one of her mother's favorite songs, the only Spanish she remembered. The air warmed and the sky shone the color of Texas bluebonnets. The little mare rounded an outcropping and there he was, riding right at her looking as if he were searching for something.

His appearance cut off her song in midstream, and she sputtered out a challenge. "What are you doing out here?"

Belle danced under her and the stallion he rode let out a coarse greeting as they stopped beside each other.

Mitch didn't want to admit that he was looking for the source of the beautiful music because it made him think of the lilt of his wife's lovely voice, the fragrance of her long black hair, the pulse in her throat at his lips. And dear God, the baby softness of their precious child's tiny body.

His reply was harsh and foolish. "Some law against it?"

A smart retort formed on her tongue, but their wandering glances caught and held and she said nothing.

He tried to make up for his earlier stupidity. "That was some pretty song you were singing. A man appreciates hearing such a thing out here in the wilderness. Lets him know there's still gentleness in the world."

Before she could reply to the totally unexpected comment, he touched the stallion's flanks and rode off.

Charlie turned to watch him disappear over the rise. He rode like he moved, with an agile grace. A man born to the saddle. The saddle and the gun.

She scolded herself for what she was thinking, for she was struck by a sudden image, herself at his side, the two of them walking hand in hand through the tall grass, happy faces kissed by the wind.

"What an utter idiot you are," she said aloud, and kicked Belle into a gallop.

Five

In the middle of the night Charlie shouted herself awake to a room awash in moonlight. Perspiration slicked her body, not from the temperature, for it was cool once the sun went down, but because of a fierce battle with some particularly wicked demons. Yet when she thought about it she couldn't remember the nightmare that had frightened her so badly. She could only imagine she heard the fading thunder of stampeding cattle. Her gown clung to her in wet patches.

The frightening dreams had begun soon after her father's death, the first of them simply a black seething cloud of fury that appeared beside her bed. A threat so real she gasped for air. For a long while she thought she had actually experienced a brush with someone or something from the other side. No doubt it was her father's anger at having been snatched from a life not yet fully lived. But why threaten her, his only beloved daughter? Of course none of it was real, and in the bright light of day she admitted that.

On many occasions since then she had screamed herself awake, and afterward wasn't sure if she'd made a sound or just dreamed that she had. Wasn't even sure she had experienced the dream.

It was always hard to get back to sleep, and so this night

she rose on shaky legs, peeled the damp gown off over her head, and padded to the window to stand bathed in the cool light of night from a half-moon. Off to her right the bunkhouse humped blackly against the glowing sky, on her left the skeletal framework of the barn threw grotesque shadows, and a line of aspen beyond drew long dark fingers across the yard.

Idly she traced a hand along the line of her jaw and down her breastbone, then caressed the swell of one breast. She closed her eyes and swayed, feeling giddy and removed from reality, as if still in the dream.

What was wrong with her? She hadn't been so conscious of her own body since the onset of puberty, but now her flesh responded to every touch and even the remotest of thoughts. Leftover fear that followed her up out of the nightmare only served to heighten that sensual awareness.

Fallon's mere presence had lit a fire, would she never extinguish it? She moved her fingers, gasped at the rigidity of her nipples, and cupped both breasts to still their aching. She wanted his hand there, his mouth, the warm satin of his tongue.

The memory of his moss-green eyes probing hers jagged through her mind like a streak of lightning cuts a storm-laden sky.

The room filled with a choking deadly panic that threatened to smother her. She whirled, hands at her throat, and gasped. Just like the dream, only this time she was awake. She had to get out, now, escape the confines of the room and breathe fresh air. She pulled on the damp gown and raced from the house as if pursued.

At the corral Belle whickered a greeting and came toward her. She scaled the fence, caught a double fistful of the roan's mane, and settled on her back, shoulders hunched against whatever invisible terror chased her.

Hair and gown flying, she urged the horse into a run, leaning forward over her neck and hanging on with both knees.

She had no idea where she was going or why, only that she had to be out in the open, had to escape the unknown dread.

Propped against a tree, his horse tethered nearby, Mitch stirred when he heard the thud of galloping hooves. He was probably less than a half mile from the Double H Ranch buildings, and had noticed no one standing night guard. Evidently when nothing more had happened after the fire, the foolish woman had begun to feel safe again. She needed someone who knew all the rules of survival to help her out or she wouldn't make it.

Ah, well, it was probably for the best if she didn't.

A thunder of hooves told him someone was coming, and coming fast. He scarcely had time to scrabble back into the shelter of the brush before the horse and rider pounded into sight.

He gaped in disbelief when the white-clad specter approached, riding like the wind. A white gown flowed along behind shapely bare legs that clamped the animal's heaving sides. The apparition rode straight at him so that he thought horse and rider might actually trample him until both turned at the last possible moment. Mitch swore he felt the breath from the roan's flared nostrils. Off to his left Jeb screamed and pawed air, but the ghost appeared oblivious.

The rider reined in at the top of the rise, silhouetted against the night sky. After a few moments the ethereal figure slid from the horse and stood illuminated by silvery moonlight. The horse dropped its nose into the grass and began to graze, as if this was nothing usual at all. For a long while the figure in white remained transfixed, unmoving.

He knew then who it was. What in the hell was the woman up to now? Mitch led Jeb out of the dense underbrush to watch. If he remained in the shadows she couldn't see him. Then his ears pricked. Someone was coming! Several someones.

She heard it too, for she turned just as a band of riders emerged above the rise and off to the right. She scrambled for the horse but made a bad go at mounting bareback. Then the riders were beside her and she could do nothing but face them.

Mitch eased into the saddle and rubbed his fingertips over Jeb's ear to soothe him.

Charlie didn't recognize the young Indians, but thought they weren't the Northern Cheyenne she was used to seeing. Sioux perhaps, renegades who refused to remain on the reservation in the Badlands. And who could blame them? Yancey insisted that one day she would regret her compassion for the savages. Perhaps now, caught out alone and defenseless like this, she should be more frightened, but she only felt foolish. What must they think of this white woman running around in the dark in her nightclothes?

The leader, a boy who looked no more than fourteen or so, slid from his pony. The others shouted and laughed, obviously egging him on to do whatever he might have in mind.

She tried to keep Belle between her and the boy, but he swatted the mare on the backside so that she moved away, and the Indian stood much too close to Charlie. She could smell his excitement, an overpowering animalistic odor, and it awoke in her at last a fear that dried her mouth and made her heart drum. What a reckless thing she'd done, coming out here alone and unarmed in the middle of the night.

She curled her fingers into fists and raised her chin to regard the young man.

He met her gaze with flashing dark eyes that said he was having a lot more fun than she was.

With a quick movement he grabbed a handful of her hair. The other boys laughed, shouted. Charlie remained very still, forcing herself not to show her fear.

With the other hand he clawed at the front of her gown and tried to rip it open. The tough fabric held and all he succeeded in doing was forcing her to her knees. The tufts of stiff grass and rock-strewn ground bit into her flesh, but she tightened her lips to keep from crying out.

More laughter.

Still she refused to put sound to her fear, though she was so frightened her head swam and her stomach churned.

The boy pulled her face toward his crotch and she punched at him, landing ineffectual blows on his iron-hard thighs and belly.

Slowly and stealthily Mitch rode right up on the braves without them sensing his presence. They were so immersed in their fun that not one of the half- dozen boys knew he was there.

He slid out his Colt and thumbed back the hammer with a deadly snick, and then they knew.

"That's enough, boys. Leave the lady alone."

Deliberately he took aim a few yards behind the one roughhousing the woman and pulled the trigger. The .44 shell exploded from the barrel of the Colt with a tremendous roar. The young Indians might not understand English, but they understood that sound.

He could tell right away they wanted to fight despite the gun, so he transferred it to his left fist and snaked the Winchester out, cocking it with one hand in a fluid singular motion. He pointed it directly at the boy on the ground.

"You first," he said and shot the boy in the arm.

The action effectively took all the bluff out of the braves, turned them into the young boys they were.

The one on the ground clutched his wound and rolled around, the others eyed Mitch in fear, eyes showing white.

Charlie scrabbled to her feet, shouting, "Don't kill them. Please don't kill them."

"Stay right where you are," Mitch ordered. "I ain't killing anybody. You all, git. Now. Take him with you." With the revolver he pointed at the boy hugging his bloody arm and glowering at him.

The young Indians seemed happy enough to do so, all the bluster gone out of them.

She watched them ride away, a mixture of terror and fury boiling up in her. Then she swung to confront the man who had rescued her. "They were only boys, you didn't have to shoot him."

"Had to make my point. They could've took us both. While I'm not used to manners it does seem a lady like you might have some. A simple thank you would do."

She spluttered, but knew he was right. She was really angry at herself for being so stupid as to ride into such a dangerous situation.

"You wander around a lot in the middle of the night in your nightclothes?" He reholstered the Colt and slipped the Winchester back into its scabbard.

The stallion danced sideways when Charlie darted for her own mount. "None of your business what I do."

"It is if I have to put my life on the line."

"Nobody asked you to." Not used to riding bareback, her efforts to mount the long-legged horse without a stirrup were meeting with very little success.

"Where the hell did you come from anyway?" He dismounted agilely to give her a hand, had spanned her waist with two strong hands before she could object.

The only thing between his touch and her flesh was the thin nightgown, but he left his hands there because to do otherwise would have been impossible. The warmth, the pulsing life against his palms, held him fast.

Charlie took in two careful deep breaths and remembered what had sent her flying across the plains in the first place.

Nightmares, longings, loneliness. And now this man's hands erupted within her a deep desire almost forgotten, and she didn't want to pull away. No matter what her good sense told her.

Instead she turned slightly and let him hold her close. The hammering of his heart vibrated, challenged the thrumming of her own.

She was naked. Unclothed beneath the thin fabric and she could feel the roughness of his jeans, the cut of his belt, every button of his shirt pressing against her hot flesh.

He put a finger under her chin and raised her face, his mouth so close it was a blur. His warm breath whispered over her cheeks, her lips... his hands trailed upward until he spanned the swell of her breasts with his thumbs and fingers.

Raw passion fed by the moonlight and her near brush with violence made her weak and she sagged with his embrace.

Mitch considered taking her, so explosive was his desire. He would lower her to the ground, pull the gown away from her lovely body, and quench his dreadful thirst for her, out here on the prairie in the quiet of night with only the moon as a witness. Her hair smelled like crisp summer apples, and her skin felt slightly moist as if she were touched by early morning dew. He bent forward, lips and tongue at her throat, and tasted tentatively of her sweetness.

She moaned, stiffened, cried out. "What are you doing? Stop, this instant."

Pushing away from his iron-hard grip, Charlie staggered against the mare's side. Where his mouth had been burned like a branding iron had seared the flesh and she rubbed at it. Cool night air filled her lungs with each gasp, until her brain cleared. What in God's name had she been thinking?

Bad enough she had ridden out alone at night so close to the Indian encampments, but to let this dangerous man get anywhere near her compounded the idiocy. She could think of nothing to say to him as she continued to rub at the spot where his tongue had lapped. So without a word she turned and vaulted onto the little horse. The sound of her breathing was harsh in the quiet night As she rode away, she and Belle cast a grotesque dancing shadow in the moonlight.

He remained where he was until she rode out of sight, then mounted quickly and kicked at Jeb's ribs, trying to ride fast enough and far enough to escape the haunting memories of the life he had lost so horribly and completely. He had to put this woman behind him as well, for he had used up all his chances at happiness. The rest of his life would be payment in kind for his vicious past, and he intended to make a good job of it.

By the time Charlie slid off the roan's back in her own corral, she was trembling violently. It had taken every ounce of her strength to ride away from the gunslinger. What had happened between them had managed to dull the danger with the Indian boys. Now she thought of that and wondered what the greater threat had been. She had certainly almost given herself to that man in black... had he in turn almost taken her? She thought so and that frightened her.

Frustrated with the conflicting thoughts, she decided that what she needed was more work to keep her mind occupied, to tire her body until it could do nothing but pass out at the end of the day. Then perhaps the bad dreams would go away, and with them her emotional tangle of feelings toward the man in black, the man who was her enemy.

For nearly a week she worked until she was exhausted, then fell into bed at the end of each day so tired she scarcely took two breaths before she was asleep. The dreams did indeed vanish, and she knew nothing until the sun awoke her each morning.

The danger from Dunkirk's men remained a continued threat

as cows were found with their throats slit and strangers were seen patrolling the periphery of the grazing land. Waiting for their chance to do more damage, perhaps even kill someone. There was always the fear that it would come to that sooner or later.

Early one morning while riding range Charlie noticed that the creek wasn't flowing like it should. Someone was messing with the water. That damn Dunkirk again.

Most of the men were in the south pasture, so she was headed in that direction when she rode up on Spotted Moon and three young braves taking charge of four longhorns.

"Morning, Miss Charlie," PJ. said. "I fetched up these steers for the injuns, like you said. But this fella here, he don't want no milk cow less'n he gets the calf too."

She grinned. Sly as a fox.

Spotted Moon eyed her closely, the corners of his lips threatening to turn up in an answering grin.

"We are grateful to Split Skirt for the beeves," Spotted Moon said gravely. "She is most generous."

She nodded. Spotted Moon had served as a tracker and guide for the U.S. Army back when there was all the trouble at the three forts along the Bozeman Trail. That had been one time when the Indian had come out the winner, forcing the army to move out of the area and abandon Forts Kearney, Smith, and Reno. A victorious Red Cloud had immediately burned Fort Kearney to the ground.

Spotted Moon had learned well from his white superiors, and was now turning that knowledge back upon the white man who had cheated his people.

She didn't blame him. "Agreed, she is being most generous."

"I too," Spotted Moon said, and nodded toward the boys. "They are becoming men. If they have to they will die to prove their bravery."

A chill washed up her spine, but she stood firm, making a similar gesture toward several of her hands looking on. "They too are brave men. It would be a shame for anyone to die because of one calf."

Spotted Moon looked right through her, his dark eyes reflecting sadness. "Many have already died because of the white man's greed. More will die because there will soon be no land and no buffalo. It matters little if we begin the fight here at your door, Split Skirt." He paused, letting that sink in, then finished, "All because of one calf."

In a flash she saw the meaning of the situation, and it had nothing to do with the cow and calf. It had to do more with pride, with dignity, with the last painful gasp of a people.

"Give them what they want," she said, inclining her head slightly toward Spotted Moon so that he could say he had won the battle in a proper way.

She dropped the reins and let Belle crop grass while the Indians and her hands corralled four steers, a milk cow and calf. The young braves cast quick looks at Charlie and she was sure one or two of them had been in the group that had accosted her the previous week. She pretended not to pay any attention as the entourage rode off, but fear warred with compassion within her. As she beheld the huge and beautiful country that surrounded her small kingdom, she was filled with the knowledge that she was taking part in something that would forever be written in the history of this country. The death of one mighty nation and the struggle toward the birth of another. And all she could think to do was cry like some weak woman.

If Spotted Moon was her enemy, then so be it, but she admired him in a way she could never admire Colonel Dunkirk, whose acts had proven him to be the more dangerous of the two. With the Indian, at least there would be honor, hers and his, even if she didn't always understand it.

She wondered why the Indian hadn't mentioned the confrontation between Fallon and the young braves earlier. He had, after all, shot one of the boys. Spotted Moon was very sly, and would use his knowledge wisely. She could never second-guess him, and so dismissed her uneasiness.

It took several minutes for her to get her mind back on the issue at hand. The lack of water in the creek. She spotted Yancey and went to tell him the bad news.

Legs hanging, Mitch sat on the edge of a drop-off and watched water back up into a basin above the hastily constructed dam. The colonel's men had finished it just before dark the previous night.

The thing wouldn't hold long. It couldn't. When all that water backed up behind it, something would give. Or maybe there'd be a gully washer up in the mountains and the sudden runoff would come racing down into the valley and just eat that dam away. It was purely a nuisance thing, but while it held Malone and Houston would have some mighty thirsty cattle on their hands. That would force them to think over their situation. Given time and equipment, the colonel could build a dam that would hold, at least through the dry summer months, and that's when it could hurt the other ranchers the worst.

The greedy old bastard was simply sending a message. For some odd reason, Mitch hoped that the small ranchers downstream ignored it and let nature take its course, but he figured they wouldn't.

Charlie Houston and her men along with some hands from Cal Malone's spread showed up around noon. Fallon rose and turned slowly, gaze gliding along the valley, past the rise and fall of land to the boulders and brush that could easily hide some of the colonel's men.

The crazy woman was just riding right into trouble. And here he was worried about her when he was supposed to take care of the colonel's interests.

Lazily he pulled his rifle from its scabbard and aimed low in front of her and her bunch. With great care he placed three shots a good hundred feet ahead of them, chopping up dust and big chunks of sod. They reined in, shouting, and soon were firing back, but he had already dropped behind the rise where Jeb waited.

He slid the Winchester back into its scabbard, mounted the black, and rode south along the low side of the ridge until he had flanked the riders. He expected them to retreat and pass his way soon, but when he heard nothing after thirty minutes or so, he picked his way cautiously back in their direction.

The noise of their work reached him long before he spotted their horses, tied in the shade. They were all involved in the brutal task of moving rock and already had cleared a portion of the dam so that water was beginning to trickle through.

Fallon glanced around quickly. Where were the colonel's men? If some of them showed up, they would probably kill someone just because it might be enjoyable.

Damn-fool woman. They were all fools, when you got right down to it. What could land be worth that they would risk their lives?

At least they'd had the sense to post three armed guards to keep lookout while the other men worked.

Fallon watched them awhile, but with each passing minute grew more nervous. He did not want to see the woman hurt, and the longer they kept at this thankless task, the more that became a possibility. He regarded the Winchester in its scabbard at his knee. Shooting at them hadn't deterred them earlier, so probably wouldn't now.

"Well, hell," he muttered under his breath, dismounted, and leading the black walked right up on the toiling men, most of whom were so involved in their work they didn't even see him.

Charlie spotted Fallon as she and P.J. grappled with a particularly stubborn chunk of rock in the crudely built dam. She turned loose her hold, P.J. shouted and sucked at a finger that got mashed when she let go, and Charlie came up the creek bank cursing.

Fallon smiled. She had a right smart tongue on her, and he admired some of the inventive names she called him. His amusement only made her more furious.

The men, unsure of exactly what was going on, since no guns had been pulled, simply stopped what they were doing and stared. A few chuckled and made comments to each other.

"Well, I suppose you're all just going to stand around like mules at fertility rites," Charlie declared when she caught them gaping, and went for the rifle on Belle's saddle.

Of course she hadn't a chance of reaching it, for Fallon and his stallion blocked the way.

"That's pretty good, mules at fertility rites," Fallon said so that only she could hear.

"Get out of my way. I'm surprised you just didn't shoot us all. That was you a while ago, wasn't it?"

"Sure was, and you notice you're all still living and breathing. But you won't be if you don't get out of here before some of Dunkirk's men come back. And they will."

"Dunkirk's men? Last I heard you could be included in that group. What're you doing, playing a game with us? Damn you, Fallon, don't you know what this place means to me... to *us*? How can you go up against honest men trying to make a place in this country? Don't you think drought and Indians and outlaws are trouble enough without men like Dunkirk and the likes of you?

"Now get your butt out of here and leave us be, you two-legged spawn of—"

He cut her off by touching her arm. "Miss Houston—"

"Don't *Miss Houston* me." It should have been a harsh demand, but instead came out like a hoarse plea for understanding. Her eyes filled but didn't overflow and she looked up at him, blinking. "How can you do this? You're not this kind of man. You can't be. If my father were alive..."

He nodded, and a great pain swelled in his chest. He looked down into her face, smeared with mud, hair plastered to her forehead and cheeks, and thought how absolutely beautiful she was. And then, immediately, what a fool he was.

A rush of water, the rumble of moving rock, interrupted their confrontation. The men began to shout and jump around, clambering up out of the bed of the creek as the dam came apart and water flowed once again onto the Double H.

"Now get the hell out of here," Fallon said harshly, turned from her, and mounted.

Charlie's heart hammered at her ribs. Damn the man. She ran to Belle, jerked the rifle out, and whirled to aim at the retreating gunslinger. Sight centered on his shoulder blades, she eased her finger over the trigger, and then just stood there till he rode out of sight, the barrel of the gun wavering in her grip.

Six

An entire week passed without retaliation from the colonel. At odd times Charlie caught herself scanning the horizon for the silhouette of the black horse and rider.

As the weather turned warmer the ranch hands renewed their complaints about lousy pickings for chuck. The men grew so tired of their own cooking they threatened mutiny. Even Ritter complained that if he had to drink one more cup of that brown gargle he was forced into brewing every morning 'cause no one else would go near the coffeepot, he was gonna hightail it for the Marias where he knew of a ranch with the best cook this side of Canada.

Charlie had to admit things were pretty bad. Then the sourdough starter ran out, a sure sign of bad trouble ahead. The worst biscuits anyone could whip up were better than none at all, and they'd all tried their hand at it. The results had ranged from heavy, hard lumps to a flapjack-looking mess that could only be eaten with a spoon, should anyone be so inclined. Anyway, no one knew what to do to keep the leavening working and so they had just kept using it till there wasn't enough left to start a day's biscuits.

Ritter made the remark that perhaps it just grew overnight, but that hadn't happened either.

Charlie was so desperate that she had almost decided to ride into Miles City and pluck someone off the street. Anyone would do. As she considered this while standing near the chuck wagon watching the men fuss and stir around like a herd about to stampede, a full-blown skirmish developed over the coffee, one of the men calling it belly wash.

"You could read a dad-blamed catalog through this stuff," came the next complaint, whereby the one doing the grousing grabbed the pot out of the fire and poured the remainder of the brew over the coals, sending up a column of smoke and ashes that set everyone to coughing.

Charlie turned away in disgust to eye the chuck wagon. At that moment it was mighty tempting to set it afire and have done with the entire episode. Chocco, that traitor of a cook who'd fled back to Texas, had fared well over the winter in a canvas tent, but she'd planned to build a cookhouse before the snow flew. If things kept up this way, it didn't look like there'd be a cook or hands to feed.

The stranger rode in while all the cowpokes were romping and stomping up a cloud of dust, as near calling it quits as they'd ever been. The shabby man dismounted his mangy-looking mule and attempted to introduce himself amid the hubbub. Ritter finally took notice and tugged at Charlie's arm. She was busy yelling into the face of Hank Bledsoe, the man who'd dumped the coffee.

"Looks like you could learn to make your own coffee instead of acting like such an ass," she hollered right up into his red face.

Bledsoe puffed up, turned more crimson. "Now, lookee here, Miss Charlie."

Ritter tugged at her shirt again and she spun around. "What do you want?"

With a large wooden spoon he'd picked up as a weapon just in case things got out of hand, Ritter pointed at the stranger.

"What do you want?" she repeated in much the same impatient tone, but this time the words were aimed at the grimy bum.

Sweeping his bedraggled hat off, the man began with precisely the wrong word for the circumstances. "Ma'am? My name is Crane Houston, and I come—"

Charlie grabbed the spoon out of Ritter's hand and threw it at the newcomer. "One more man calls me ma'am on this place and you're all fired, and I mean it," she shouted, and trounced off to the house.

"Hell, dressing like a man hasn't done me one whit of good. How did he know I was a ma'am anyway?" she chanted as she marched. "I don't dress like one, I don't look like one, I don't walk like one. Why does everyone call me ma'am?" She turned around, walking backward, even went so far as to shake a fist in the air, much to her chagrin. "You're all fired. Every last one of you. Fired. Do you hear me?"

Without missing a step, she whirled, stomped up onto the porch and inside the cabin, slamming the door so hard it bounced back open.

She sat down at the table, got up and walked a circle, plopped on the edge of the bed. "If I had a dress, I swear I'd put it on about now, let some man take over this mess and straighten it out."

Having come up with the idea amazed her. Stunned, she sat for a while thinking over what had happened. She had acted just like a woman. Men and women were different in their reactions to situations. A man...her father, would have settled that uprising out there in a split second without flouncing off like a spoiled child. He might even have punched someone in the mouth, but he would have gotten the job done. Six months ago, that's precisely what she would have done too. What was going on?

Someone cleared his throat and she looked up to see the stranger standing in the open doorway, hat in both hands. Why did men always hold their hats right there across their middle, like they were protecting something precious? She giggled and covered her mouth. Again, just like a woman. She threw her shoulders back and stood as tall as she could, an impressive five feet eight in her boots.

That's when she realized with a start that the man had said his name was Houston.

"Did you say *Houston*?"

The man nodded and raised an eyebrow. He was a little taller than her, fairly broad in the shoulders, with a mustache and several days growth of salt and pepper beard. He wasn't handsome, but he wasn't ugly either. Just quite ordinary, very scruffy, and nothing at all like her father, the only other Houston she had ever known, besides herself, of course. This one was disappointingly down on his luck.

"Are you Matt's girl?" he finally asked. He had a friendly voice and his faded blue eyes sparkled like he appreciated the humor in the scene he had ridden into. There might have been a little bit of Matt there, she wasn't sure.

"I'm Charlie. Charlotte Maria Houston. Do I know you?"

"Probably not, you were very small when I saw you last. When I left Texas. As I said, my name's Crane, Crane Houston. I'm your very own cousin, your daddy's eldest brother's only boy."

The strange man's announced family tie sent an odd feeling of pleasure through her. He was kin. A precious link to her father.

"Oh, come in, please do." She strode to the bed, straightened the coverlet, gestured toward the chairs around the table, the only other place to sit unless you chose the floor.

"Where did you come from? I mean, how did you get here? How did you find me?"

The man sat where she indicated, dropped his disreputable hat on the floor, and folded his hands together on the table in front of him.

Black dirt rimmed the nails, but that didn't matter. She hovered over him, suddenly eager to make a connection. "Are you hungry, could I get you something to eat?"

Crane glanced pointedly in the direction of the chuck wagon outside and smiled. "I don't think so, but maybe I could get you something to eat. And them too."

Her mouth dropped open, the announcement rendered her speechless. Surely such things didn't happen. It was like making a wish and having the genie appear.

He went on. "I mean, I learned to cook pretty good when I... uh, well, while I was on my own. A feller gets down on his luck he learns lots of things."

"Uh, well, some may," she replied. "Those yahoos out there would starve before they'd learn how to cook. It isn't proper for a cowboy to know how to cook. Cowboys only know how to tell the front end of a cow from the ass end, that's all cowboys know. And how to sit a bronc so they can ride out on a Saturday night and poke every soiled dove within a thousand miles. That's all cowboys know." She neglected to mention her own shortcomings in that area.

Crane widened his eyes and had the decency to look embarrassed. "You're upset, maybe I should just mount up and ride on. I didn't intend to cause you worry."

"Upset? Yes. Don't go, please, Mr. Houston, I mean Crane, I mean cousin."

"Crane is fine," he said. He stood, pointed toward the door. "Why don't I just go out there and see what I can do? Would that be okay?"

She let out a tremendous sigh. "Dear God, yes, that would

be okay... Crane. And thank you. Thank you from the very bottom of my heart."

He stopped at the door and turned to study her. "Oh, there's no need for thanks. I expect you'll pay me cook's wages, just like any other hand. Won't you?"

There was a look in the man's eyes that she found puzzling. She would remember it later. Right now all she knew was that this man, this cousin, had rescued her in what her father would have called the ginger nick of time.

She followed him to the door, but not out to the chuck wagon. In no time he had donned an apron and started putting things right.

It wasn't long before Yancey Barton separated himself from the cluster of watchful cowboys and strolled up to the cabin. She stepped out and sat on the top step, grinning widely at him.

"Well, you musta been at the cream pitcher, with that look," he said, and sat down beside her.

She hugged her knees and rocked backward. "It's a miracle."

"Well, now, ain't you just too tickled with yourself, Charlie? Who is that, anyway?"

"You don't need to sound so grumpy. He saved our bacon, showing up when he did. And look, he's already got breakfast cooking. Just smell that meat sizzling...and the coffee boiling."

Yancey eyed her for a long while, shook his head, and crammed his hat down over his brow. "Don't suppose you asked for any references."

"No. And there was no need. That's my daddy's own kin out there. That's Crane Houston."

"So he told us. Looks like nothing but a chuck-line saddle bum to me. Why didn't I ever hear of this feller? Your daddy tell you of this feller, did he?"

Something went thud in her stomach. Matt had never told

her about any kin. All she knew was his long-time affiliation with the King Ranch. Richard King had been her "uncle," and her mother's many relatives in both Texas and Mexico the only family she knew. Was Yancey only trying to stir up trouble or did he have a point?

"You can't get me down, Yancey. You're always looking for the worst in everyone. You're not getting away with it this time. Saddle bums just come begging to belly up at the chuck wagon. Most of them don't offer to do the cooking. Besides, why would the man make up such a story as that? How would he know about me and my father?"

"Oh, yeah? And just what did he know?"

She thought about that for a while. It was true. He hadn't even mentioned Matt's brother's name. Not that it would have helped her any. The realization made her impatient with her ramrod's cynical common sense.

"Never you mind, Yancey, you just go take care of your business and I'll take care of mine. Put those men to work when their bellies are full, and forget all this nonsense."

He rose, hooked his thumbs in his waistband, and said, "Yes, sir, Miss Charlie. Anything else?" But his eyes were sparkling, and she knew he was only teasing. She and Yancey Barton had never had harsh words over anything, just like he and Matt had never argued seriously.

"No, nothing else. Get over there and eat something yourself, you're entirely too puny."

He loped off without saying anything else, but his earlier questions left a stale taste in her mouth, one she was hard-put to wash away, even with a cup of the excellent coffee Crane Houston served up at the chuck wagon a little while later.

❀

Mitch rode to the Circle D Ranch late that evening in response to the colonel's summons. Out in the corral a couple of rough riders were finishing off a new string of wild horses, and some of the hands sat around atop the rail fence shouting and cussing encouragement with a certain flavoring of derision. In reality the men watching might well be ranch hands, but that wasn't what they were hired for. The more men the colonel hired, the more Mitch wished he could just move on. This was shaping up to be all-out war, and he'd almost rather head for the hills as take part. But he was committed, and besides it kept his mind off darker thoughts. Lately he'd been troubled by a terrible yearning to connect with family, be with people he knew. There was only one, his sister Dessa, off somewhere with her husband Ben Poole making tons of money, he'd heard. He had a mighty urge to ride back down to Missouri and rest his bones in the old family home place. Hard to figure what brought that on.

He was surprised to see Colonel Dunkirk seated atop a buckboard that had been pulled up to the fence, watching the horse breaking as if it were pure entertainment.

"Over here, Fallon," the colonel shouted when Mitch swung from his saddle. "A couple more men I want you to meet. So's we don't go killin' our own when the shootin' starts." The fat man held his belly and guffawed.

Mitchell tilted his black Stetson forward a bit to cut the harsh glare of the late afternoon sun and approached the corral. A great shout went up as a rider clawed sky bouncing off a wild bronc bent double and airborne. The man hit the ground on his butt, grunted, and picked himself up. He walked stiffly toward the kicking, screaming horse.

"Git 'im, Utah. Hell's bells, he ain't nothin' but a bolt of lightning," someone shouted.

All the men along the fence laughed.

The colonel ignored the horseplay and gestured toward two men who stood straddle-legged, one hand on the butts of their side arms, steely eyes aimed at Mitch.

"This here's Cross 'n Neddy. Boys, this is Fallon."

Cross nodded in a lank-jawed manner, a lock of dirty blond hair falling down between his close-set gray eyes, as flat and unyielding as gunmetal. He wore a fancy silver belt buckle as big as his hand. His pal Neddy grinned, dimples bloomed, and he looked for all the world like someone's sweet little fifteen-year-old grandson with fat rosy cheeks and a well-fed body. A new and dangerous brand of outlaw was discovering the territories lately, men who had been too young to serve in the war and had purely self-serving axes to grind.

Mitch nodded curtly, didn't offer a hand, neither did they. Hands belonged on the butts of pistols, not tied up in someone else's fist, and he rested his where it was meant to be just like they did.

The colonel stood in the buckboard and nodded at his bodyguard, the ugly, scar-faced man everyone called Wolf because his eyes looked just like a predator's. The man promptly let go a shrill whistle that not only spooked the horses, but brought every man jack on the fence to attention.

"Colonel wants you all in the study, pronto," Wolf announced, helped his boss down from the seat, and escorted him toward the ranch house.

Mitch had never quite gotten over some of the terms the scarcely literate Wolf used when following the colonel's commands. He obviously picked them up from his boss and was proud to show how he could use them. The word study wouldn't be in his vocabulary otherwise. To him it was a room in a house. There was a big shiny desk, bookshelves filled with leather-bound books, and plenty of chairs for the frequent meetings the colonel held there plotting how he would steal his next parcel of land.

Some things in this life were hard to figure out, like how come a man like the colonel was allowed to live on to bedevil everyone while someone like his Celia and sweet innocent little Fawn had to die so horribly. There were times when Mitch toyed with just shooting the old son of a bitch and putting everyone out of his misery. Then, provided Wolf didn't gun him down on the spot, the law could hang him and everything would be all done with.

He picked a chair near the bank of windows where he could look out on the yard and corrals. The position also gave him a good view of the approach road to the ranch itself. He always half expected someone to come riding in looking for him. After all those years following the war when he ran from one hiding place to the other, sometimes just a jump ahead of the law and a hanging rope, every holdup in the territory laid at his feet. The dreaded Yank, many times compared to Quantrill, was thought to be dead, though. Some said he had been killed in a gun battle with Sheriff Moohn out at Alder Gulch near Virginia City. And his sister Dessa and her husband Ben Poole the only ones who knew he and Celia had escaped that fatal gun battle. Yank had died, but only in spirit. Mitch became a different man, a loving husband and father. Now he was none of those, now he was nothing. A man with no life, no love, no connections.

Why the hell didn't he just leave Montana and go somewhere else? Well, by God maybe he just would. For a running dead man, one place was just as good as another.

The colonel interrupted his musings. "What the hell, Fallon, you going to join us or gape off into thin air?"

Mitch swiveled away from the window. For two bits he'd walk away from this crazy man's army, ride out of Montana, and never look back. But he couldn't. Something held him here that he didn't quite understand. It had to do with the woman, and that's all he knew for sure.

The colonel addressed the men. "It's time to put an end to this nonsense. We'll run 'em all out or bury 'em where they fall, either way they're leaving my land. Starting tonight I want hit-and-run raids. Quick and fast, in and out. Make believers out of them. I'd rather they'd pull up stakes and leave, less questions to answer. If they don't, well, the law around here is bought and paid for. There are five small ranches and three families of sodbusters on my land and I want rid of them, once and for all.

"I've found most men are easily scared bad enough to run if you give them the room to do it. Back 'em up against a wall and some will turn and fight. I'd rather see 'em run, but if you can't...." He hunched his thick shoulders. A tacit and unspoken permission to kill with his blessings.

When no one said anything, he looked straight at Mitch, then shifted to Cross, then on to Neddy. One by one he made eye contact with the men gathered around the desk.

"All right, I think I've made myself clear," he said.

The men all nodded, ready to do his bidding, no matter what it was. He had bought and paid for their guns. Now he was asking for results, and he would get them.

Mitch shifted uncomfortably. It was one thing to shoot at someone who was bound to shoot you, but this harassing settlers, struggling ranchers, women, and kids. It riled his better judgment.

Just ordinary folk. Ordinary folk. Done nothing to deserve what the Colonel had in mind for them, except try to hold on to what was theirs.

Mitch squeezed his eyes shut. What a fool. It was ordinary folk that stood by while others like them murdered his wife and child. There was no reason except that they were Indian, different, frightening to white men who were stealing land that rightfully belonged to the Sioux.

He'd tried to wipe the blood from her face, tenderly unfastened the board that held the silent Fawn, knelt beside them, clutching their limp bodies to his chest, rocking and screaming like a mortally wounded animal.

And the men, their horses prancing around the bloody sight, good men and true. Innocent men. White men. Men just like Cal Malone and Matt Houston and Duffy McGrew and all the rest.

"Git yourself another squaw, squaw man. Before we kill ever' last one of 'em, wipe 'em off the face of the earth. Bloody savages," one yelled over the body of his dead wife and child.

Mitch ground his teeth and opened his eyes. So real had been the images that he was shocked to find himself in the colonel's study. The stench of death and sweat and anguish followed him into the room, and it took a moment to orient himself. What difference did it make who he killed? What difference indeed? There were no innocents in this land.

Then why... dear God, why did he say what he did and put himself up against it? "I'll take care of the Houston place, and I won't need any help."

The colonel produced a malicious smirk. "See you do. I'm spread thin, surely anyone can take care of a woman and a few scraggly hands."

Charlie padded around in her socks, glancing out first one window, then the other. The music box tinkled, but her enjoyment was lost to a restlessness she couldn't quite explain.

She went to one of the windows and loosened the tanned deer hide stretched over the opening to let in some night air.

There were only three windows in the small cabin and over each she had stretched the beautiful deer hides, tanned fine by the Cheyenne women so that the lamplight glowed through them. Spotted Moon's wife had given them to her the winter afternoon when she had held the woman's child close to her barren breasts.

Things were going well, the ranch had a cook, Dunkirk had backed off, so she couldn't explain the way she felt. On edge, as if waiting for something wonderful or frightening to happen. When the disk stopped playing she put the music box away. In another moment she moved from the window and twirled through the room on her toes, making three graceful circles before coming up against the bed.

How she missed Matt. The winter had been tough but she'd thought that once through it she would be okay. Now that spring was here the loneliness had deepened into a steady burning ache that no amount of hard work would soothe. She missed working at his side, sensing his manly strength, sharing his love for a hard day's labor.

With a deep sigh she stepped out onto the porch, leaving the door ajar at her back so that a pool of light lay around her.

It was pure carelessness that got him caught. Mitch had ridden fairly close to the cabin and was sitting there taking in the view as shamelessly as some kid when that young man he'd seen around the ranch walked right up on him.

Jeb sensed the man's presence and tried to telegraph it to his master, but Mitch ignored the stallion's antics.

The gruff order, "Stay right where you are, mister," was the first Mitch knew anybody was around except him and the lovely Miss Houston, who liked to dance when alone, it seemed.

He wasn't too worried that the man would shoot him, but he felt foolish all the same. Besides, he wasn't too sure about Charlie

Houston. She might just as soon shoot him as look at him, especially after he'd been caught sneaking around in the dark.

"Now you climb down off a that there horse and if you even have to sneeze, don't, 'cause I'm not very good with this old rifle and sometimes it goes off when I'm not looking."

Mitch kept his hands high and swung agilely off Jeb. It was pretty dark, but not so much so that he could get away with anything.

"Miss Charlie. Yancey. Get yourselves out here, I done caught me a coyote."

The man's shouting caused Jeb to bolt into the darkness. "Traitor," Mitch muttered.

"Shut up, mister,"

Yancey arrived first, waving around a rifle. "Well, Ritter, good work. What was he up to?"

"Just sitting his horse looking in at Miss Charlie. He wasn't doing anything."

"Probably fixing to, though. Come back to finish what you started and burn us out?" Yancey glared at Fallon.

Charlie had stomped into her boots as she clamored off the porch and came on the scene late. When she saw Fallon under the guns of both Ritter and Yancey she yelled at them without thinking. "Don't shoot him, for God's sake."

Yancey turned toward her. "I don't reckon we had that in mind exactly, Charlie. The thing is, what do you want us to do with him?"

She stepped closer so she could look up into Fallon's face. "Why is it every time I turn around I run into you? You're the dangdest excuse for a gunslinger I ever saw."

"He was watching you through the window yonder," Ritter said and gestured toward the cabin.

Charlie glanced in that direction and felt heat creeping up

her throat. with the lamps lit he could see her right through those hides. "You mangy coward, you double-butted, red-eyed—"

"Now, Charlie, whoa now," Yancey said. "Don't go getting yourself in an uproar. You'll only say something that'll embarrass you when you go to thinking on it. This here fella ain't worth that. Think what your daddy would've done."

"He'd have thrashed him soundly and made him walk home bare-ass naked," she said.

"Sounds good to me," Ritter said. "You hold the gun, Yancey, while I take care of this matter."

Fallon made a rude sound down in his throat and Charlie darted a quick look at him. It would take more than two men to accomplish such a feat, she was sure. Perhaps even Matt Houston couldn't have gotten the job done. Besides, she didn't like the idea, miffed as she was about him skulking around.

"I apologize for staring in at you, Miss Houston," Fallon said, the first words he'd uttered since he'd climbed down off Jeb. "I came by to warn you that the colonel is going to step up his attack on the small ranchers. I'm sorry but I caught sight of you through the shade and couldn't help but look. I never saw a rancher dance quite like that before. It's a rare sight out here on the plains."

She caught a hint of humor in the gruff voice. "Don't you dare laugh at me."

"I meant nothing but to pay you a compliment."

A strange emotion filled her throat and she turned away from the three men. "Let him go. Get out of here, Fallon, and don't come back. Next time you're liable to be shot for the killer you are."

"But, Miss Charlie," Ritter said.

"Aw, hell, Charlie," Yancey added.

"Shut up, both of you. And you, Fallon, you shut up too. No more fawning and skulking around. Stay out of my sight, forever." She walked away and didn't look back.

Seven

For a while Cal Malone was content to consider the ruckus a part of his dream, so it was several minutes before he awoke enough to realize that the shots he heard might be real. When a bullet whined through the ranch house and shattered a lamp before thudding into the wall beside his bed, he knew.

This was no dream.

He kicked away the tangled blanket, leaped from the bed, grabbed up his Spencer. Disregarding his lack of proper clothing—he preferred to sleep in his union suit bottoms—Cal burst onto the porch in time to see two riders disappear into the darkness south of the ranch house.

Damn that colonel! If the man was bent on war, then by God he would oblige him.

Racing barefoot across the yard, Cal vaulted up top of the corral fence and over onto the bare back of one of his cow ponies. Without considering the futility of chasing after riders in the dark, he bumped loose the top rail of the fence, urged the pony over the bottom one, and headed south in hot pursuit of the fleeing raiders.

Odd they hadn't ridden north back toward the Circle D, but Cal didn't stop to ponder on that too long either. He would catch them if he had to ride till sunrise. Could be they were going to hit every rancher in the area in one night. He rode for maybe half an hour without seeing anything but silent stands of juniper and pine. Finally he reined in the chuffing, sweating horse. No sense killing a good mount. He'd never catch them in the dark anyway. Having ridden away most of his anger, Cal decided he might as well go home.

Disappointment at not catching at least one of the riders in his gunsights rode with him as he headed back toward the Rocking R. He'd like that colonel to meet him face-to-face like a man. The dirty rotten coward, sending out gun hands to harass hardworking men who were doing nothing but trying to make a living.

Be damned if he'd give up the land that he and Becky had toiled over, sacrificed everything for. His beloved wife had given her life, and he wasn't about to let a bunch of paid-for guns drive him off. They would bury him on the hill at her side before he'd let that happen.

Thus engaged, Cal didn't hear the shot or feel the bullet that caught him in the throat. Surprise flooded over him as he toppled off the horse and landed on the ground flat on his back.

What the hell was he doing staring up at the night sky?

There was no pain. In awe, he watched a soft glow fade into the darkness, and wondered just what kind of strange dream this was, anyway.

"Becky," he murmured. "Becky, don't cry."

And she smiled and held out her arms to him.

The next afternoon about four o'clock Cal's foreman Zeke rode into the yard at the Double H. Charlie was swamping out the new barn because all the men were out on the range except Ritter, and he was off somewhere gathering firewood. At the thrum of hoof-beats she dropped the shovel and went to meet the rider, expecting more trouble just because that's the way things were going. Chickens scattered around her feet, squawking and pecking at the ground. On the move she pulled her gloves off and rolled her shoulders to chase away a cramp. When she saw the morose face of the Rocking R's ramrod, goose bumps trickled after a trail of sweat down her back.

"What's happened?" Her dry throat caught at the words.

He dismounted with the horse in motion. "It's Cal. He's been shot."

A familiar jag of pain lanced through her and she covered her mouth to keep from crying out, then asked, "How bad is he?" Without waiting for a reply she ran for the tack room.

Zeke trotted along beside her. "Bad. Real bad. I'm sorry to say Cal's dead. We found him around dawn. The colonel sent some men to hurrah the place and Cal rode out after them. Damnedest thing, he was only wearing his drawers and carrying a Spencer. Didn't even saddle up. In all the commotion I never even seen him ride out. Damnedest thing."

Tears burned at her eyes as she pulled a bridle, saddle, and blanket off the rack. "Oh, poor Cal. Isn't that just like him? He's *dead*? How did it happen? I mean, where... how... *who*?" She knew what she was really asking was did Mitchell Fallon have anything to do with her friend's death. Did he ride from here directly over there and shoot Cal?

She would kill him, lie in wait behind some rock and put a bullet between his eyes. Hate lurked dark and ugly inside her, the taste bitter in her mouth.

At the same time her lips wouldn't form the question of Zeke. Did you see a man all dressed in black, riding a wild black stallion? Did he then follow Cal and shoot him down?

No, she couldn't ask. She desperately didn't want Fallon involved, wanted him to be innocent. His touch tamed her soul, and that was enough of a reason.

Zeke rattled on. "Out by Butcher's Holler, there where them big rocks are? We figure they laid in wait for him, gunned him down from ambush. He never fired a shot. His horse come in is why we rode out looking at all. Otherwise, you know, Cal would sometimes ride off a mad. Since Miss Rebecca died he's been that way. Ride half the night just staring off in the distance, like he might could catch up with her if he went far enough."

Charlie slowed in her trek to the corral and threw the foreman a look. Sometimes men said the most surprising things. You'd go along and go along, thinking they were just hard-riding, cussing, spitting, drinking, simple men, and then one would say something insightful and catch you unawares.

The man eyed her back, then looked down at his feet. "Reckon he finally did, huh?"

Tears poured over her cheeks as she hurried to the corral to saddle up. Poor Cal. Those sons of bitches would pay. Whether it was Fallon or someone else, this time they would pay. They'd gone too far, shooting Cal Malone, and by God, something would be done if she had to ride to Virginia City and fetch the territorial marshal herself. Someone should have done it long ago and not waited for one of the best men she knew to get gunned down. Who would have thought, though, that the colonel would go this far? As it turned out, he hadn't backed off after they dynamited the dam, he had simply reconnoitered and come at them again, in his own time with his own rules.

Tightening the cinch on the prancing roan, Charlie said, "Ride to the other ranches, fetch Duffy and Lester Burris and that dandy Basil Hawthorne and the others. I'm going to town to see what can be done about this. Tell them to meet me there at the sheriff's office."

With the man trotting at her heels Charlie went to the house and fetched her Winchester. She hesitated just long enough to make sure it was loaded, then hurried back to her saddled horse.

"What about Cal, Miss Charlie?"

She mounted, tugged the mare's head around, and stared down at him. "What about him? He's dead."

"But he'll need a burying."

"Yes, he will indeed need a burying, but not right now. It'll wait till tomorrow. I'll stop at the undertaker's and arrange things. Cal would want to be buried with Rebecca on the ranch."

She kicked the horse and rode off, the wind drying her tears so that her cheeks grew stiff.

Most of the colonel's ranch lay to the north of the Double H, but the ranch house itself was built in the crook of the Porcupine Creek after it flowed off Charlie's land and back onto a section of the colonel's land. Her ranch house and his weren't far apart as distance was judged in the sprawling Montana Territory.

Miles City lay to the south on the Powder River before it ran into the Yellowstone, but she detoured to the colonel's first because she could do nothing else. Grief at the loss of a friend, anger that one man could get away with such a terrible thing as murder, the stubbornness she'd inherited from Matt Houston, all teamed up on her to prevent her doing the smart thing and riding straight into Miles City.

The ranch was unusually quiet when she rode in. The roan slowed, blowing from being galloped hard, and she left her at the hitching rail by the porch. In the eerie silence her boots thunked noisily when she crossed the wide planks.

She pounded on the mammoth door with the flat of her hand. "Colonel, you better git yourself out here." With the toe of one boot she kicked the door a couple more times. "Open up, now, you no-good, back-shooting son of a—"

"Whoa," a voice said right at her shoulder.

She whirled to see Mitchell Fallon leaning up against a pillar, a frown creasing his broad forehead.

For a moment neither spoke, just studied each other like hunter and prey.

Finally she broke the silence. "Where is that damned murdering bastard?"

Something flashed in his eyes. A threat? "You ought to ride on your way. This could get you killed."

"Like it got Cal Malone killed? Is that how, Fallon? Did you pull the trigger on my friend, shoot him down in cold blood? All because he wanted something to call his own? Tell me, what makes a man like you able to live with himself? How do you sleep nights? How do you even get out of bed of a morning, knowing today you're going to go out and murder someone else? Just how does that work?

"Dear God, I wish I'd have let Ritter and Yancey at you last night. I should have shot you myself."

His green eyes batted as if she'd slapped him, and Charlie could have sworn she saw a hint of compassion before his features closed down. He straightened and rested the heel of his right hand on his pistol butt. "Like I said, ride out."

As he spoke a handful of men rounded the corner of the ranch house, all headed in their direction.

She glanced at them, anxiety leaching away her fury. "Oh, I will. And you tell your precious colonel that I intend to bring in the territorial marshal. This is murder, pure and simple. There'll be no self-defense. You've gone too far this time."

Mitch watched Charlie walk away, her gait stiff and unnatural. He wished she hadn't mentioned the marshal in the other men's hearing. She was barely holding it together, and he wanted to chase after her, tell her he had nothing to do with this. The hate smoldering in her incredible dark eyes, the way her soft, full lips tightened into a sneer of disgust, pained him. He didn't want her feeling that way about him.

That arrogant Cross and his murderous sidekick had done precisely what Mitch had been afraid of and killed Cal Malone. A range war was one thing, but out-and-out laying-in-wait killing quite another. Only in war had Mitch done something so loathsome, no matter the target. Whatever happened now would serve the colonel right.

Ignoring the gun hands and their questions about what was going on, Mitch hurried to the bunkhouse where he threw his meager belongings into his canvas poncho, cinched it up, and headed for the corral. There he saddled the stallion, tied on the bedroll, slid his Winchester into the scabbard, and mounted up. Out of sight of the ranch house he hesitated for a moment, unsure of which direction to ride. Then he headed west, following the trail that meandered alongside Porcupine Creek.

He had seen a stubbornness in the Houston woman's eyes that reminded him of something he'd struggled to forget. He'd seen that same harsh determination in Celia's eyes more than once, a hardheaded resolve that had finally gotten her killed. He hadn't been able to stop her from doing the things she simply had to do. Like walking openly in the streets of Bismarck with her half-white baby, while her people ravaged the Badlands slaughtering the white men who were destroying their way of life for the sake of railroads and gold.

He should never have brought his wife and child back into the territories after they'd fled to Canada.

But she missed her family so, longed for the Dakota land from where she'd come, dreamed of presenting a grandchild to her mother and father. All those years of running with the outlaw bands after the war had made Celia tough and unyielding, and he couldn't stand up to her once she'd made up her mind. Hell, he'd loved her, so how could he deny her such a simple request as to go home to her people? The pain in his heart cut so cruelly that he wished he could forget those few years he'd spent with a woman who adored him, who bore him a child, who gave him hope. Just slash the memory out of his brain as viciously as Cross had slaughtered Malone. Then maybe all he'd have left would be an empty loneliness and no expectations of anything better.

This woman, this Charlie Houston, who dressed like a man and acted like one, had a stubborn streak that he judged would get her killed too. He wasn't going to stay around and watch it happen, and he sure as hell wasn't going to be a part of it.

He rode on, shutting out everything but his need to be gone. Before all hell busted loose he could ride right into the sun as it set in the west. He could be in Idaho Territory before Charlie Houston died, if he rode hard.

Charlie sat outside the sheriff's office on the end of the boardwalk, waiting for the other ranchers to show up. The sheriff wasn't around, nor was his crazy deputy everyone called Acorn because he was so squirrelly.

The colonel was right when he said the only law in Miles City was what he himself allowed. How could the small ranchers hope to get anything accomplished? Why did those filthy killers have to go and shoot Cal? To scare the rest of them, maybe? To say that if they didn't give in and sell out to the colonel, this is what would happen to all of them?

She smacked the edge of her fist down on the weathered wood. Well, it wasn't going to be so easy. It wasn't going to happen because she wouldn't let it.

The men she'd sent Zeke after rode into town some time later. Her own ramrod Yancey Barton was with them, his face a picture of concern.

It didn't take long to weed out those who would fight

for their land from those who wouldn't. The snobbish Basil Hawthorne would sell out and return to England, the rest would stay, but a couple were on the fence. Charlie sensed that when it came to push and shove, they'd sell too. She was pretty sure the rest would stick it out.

When she brought up the territorial marshal, the men scoffed.

"And when was the last time you seen him around Miles City?" McGrew asked. "It'll take a while to find him, I'd wager. In the meanwhile we need a plan."

And so it was finally decided that McGrew would send a man to hunt down the marshal, the rest would draw their battle lines. Together they would stand hard against Colonel Dunkirk and his hired guns the best way they knew.

Zeke decided to ride to Virginia City and claim Cal Malone's place before the colonel beat him to it. Zeke had been ramrod for Cal from the very beginning. Everyone agreed and Zeke left. He would miss Cal's funeral, but the rancher would have understood the need for haste.

Charlie sat on the porch long after dark that night, the rifle lying beside her. Yancey had sent two men in off the range for night guard, one was in the loft of the new barn, the other in the bunkhouse. At dawn they would sleep and two more would take their place.

To keep the men from growing careless, all pairs would rotate watching the ranch and riding the range, with everyone getting his share of sleep and range work mixed in with guarding. Yancey had devised a fair schedule.

Sleep proved elusive, and the later it got the more restless she grew. She had ridden in hot and dusty, needing a bath. After a late three-quarter moon crept into the sky she rose from the porch, went inside for a bar of soap and towel and her nightgown. Then she strolled down to the creek breathing deeply of the pine-scented air and the lingering animal aroma that told her she was exactly where she belonged, even in the face of all the trouble.

Mitch's trip to Idaho had gotten him as far as the banks of the Porcupine within hearing distance of the Double H Ranch. There he bedded down for the night. He was in no particular hurry to get to Idaho. He had set up a cold camp and chewed on jerky and hardtack from his pack, then settled back where he could see the light in the woman's cabin through the dense thicket.

Her silent passage through the brush alerted his sensitive hearing, and he crept on his hands and knees toward the sound.

It was late and a full moon crept up from the eastern horizon to illuminate the land. A stand of willows threw umber shadows down the rise to her left, and ahead, thick poplars and box elder stood in silent, dark splendor. Leaves rustled underfoot and the brush crackled as she made her way to the water's edge.

Far off, the bawling of cattle had faded to low, soothing moans as the herd pastured nearby settled for the night.

On his knees, Mitchell gazed in unexpected anticipation through the branches heavy with pungent foliage. At the edge of the creek Charlie Houston shed the trappings of her tough cattle-droving life. She tossed the wide-brimmed dusty hat over a skeletal branch, gleaming in a splash of moonlight, removed the sweat-stained bandanna, and draped it nearby. The stiff-dried Kentucky jeans slumped like discarded skin against the tree's thick trunk. She stood naked, a gentle breeze stirring goose bumps along the curve of her back where it rounded into supple hips and long, lean thighs.

Crouched in silence he caught his breath at the vision that emerged from her cowpunchers cocoon like a moon moth.

Golden light splintered across the still water, reflected around her to caress erect nipples, a tight, flat stomach, the shadowy secret nested below. Tendrils of white curled from the water's surface into the chilly air and she waded deeper into the creek, disturbing the rising mist. Her face remained in darkness, the shoulder-length hair reflected bits of gold like a shattered halo.

Whatever gods ruled over his life were once again tantalizing him, and he wanted to cry out. A savage "No" ripped from deep in his gut but made not a sound.

He couldn't have this woman, he shouldn't want her, yet he couldn't stop his desire any more than he could ride away from her troubles. No woman was more vulnerable than when she was naked, and he was ashamed of spying on her yet he couldn't turn away. For an instant, though, he closed his eyes, and when he opened them her supple buttocks were sinking into the silvery surface as she lowered herself until only her shoulders and head were above water.

How silken and soft that skin would feel beneath the roughness of his fingertips. How sweet her flesh would taste and smell. When he held her, the fine strands of hair would spill over his chest and tickle his nose as he bent to kiss the top of her head. He knew how she smelled, how she felt, what it was like to hold her, and he felt a great loss because she wasn't in his arms. A moan surged from his throat and he suppressed it for fear he would frighten her away and be alone again.

Graceful hands clutching a bar of soap, she massaged up her throat and across both shoulders. He imagined smoothing the fragrant bar over her back in gentle circles until she broke out in goose bumps, turned, and came into his arms.

Her bare breasts would press against his chest, the firm nipples tantalizing him until he lowered his head and took first one, then the other into his mouth.

Dear God, what was happening to him?

Had he gone crazy, round the bend crazy like he'd heard

about when men remained too long alone in such a empty expanse of land?

It didn't matter that he might be going nuts, he couldn't budge. He remained frozen in time and watched while she washed her hair. She lifted both arms so that her breasts floated on the water, the nipples peeking right at him where he hunkered in the brush like some kind of primitive animal.

As she laced fingers through her hair a pleasant but very disturbing heat swelled between her loins. A tickling sensation tiptoed over her breasts and she was filled with a profound desire such as she had never known.

Disturbed by the wanton feelings and a small sound from the brush, Charlie scampered from the water, dropped her gown over her head, and hurried back to the cabin.

She thought of Mitchell Fallon and how he'd lurked out in the dark and watched her. No man had ever looked at her quite like he did. He seemed to be trying to puzzle out some great dark secret with a gaze that penetrated her very soul. Every time she was caught up by those magnetic green eyes though, they would frost over like glass on a cold night.

Mitchell watched the woman drift across the moon-splashed meadow grass like a ghost in the ethereal white gown. He waited awhile after she went inside the cabin, hoping she would light a lamp and he could catch a glimpse of her shadow crossing the window openings. But she didn't, and after a while he crept silently back to his camp. He remained very quiet, stealthy even, for he hadn't missed her acknowledging wave that told him someone was keeping lookout besides himself. He'd have to watch his step or they might shoot him for the trespasser that he was.

Eight

Thunder woke Charlie, sending her scurrying out of bed to tie down the window coverings that flapped in a brisk wind. She thought of Cal and his funeral planned for this morning. For some reason it never failed to rain on a burying.

Just like that horrible day on the trail when they'd buried her father, the howling wind, the icy pellets of rain, men huddled around in ponchos like hovering specters, rivulets of water pouring into the yawning hole before they could shovel the mud onto the canvas-wrapped body.

She shuddered, forced away the memory, and climbed back in bed to snuggle deeper under the covers for a few minutes. Death came on such awesome feet and at the most inopportune of times. But then, when was a good time to greet such an unwelcome visitor?

Outside horses whinnied and men shouted and the ranch came awake for another day. With a sigh of dread she rose, dressed quickly, and stepped out onto the porch. Before moving through the water cascading in sheets off the roof, she pulled the poncho tight around her neck. It was time to say good-bye to Cal.

Standing around the grave, the men kept their hats on to shield themselves from the worst of the deluge.

The rain looked like it had settled in for a long stay. That was the way of this country. Dry as a bone till you thought you'd choke, then it'd come a toad strangler that floated everything away. The month of June was moving on. When this rainy spell passed, there wouldn't likely be another all summer.

Charlie welcomed the moisture for the pastures, but she couldn't help wishing the sun had shone for Cal's funeral. A dreary send-off to offer such a fine man. Even the distant mountains wore somber shrouds.

Around the grave, someone said a few words. She paid little attention to them. What mattered was her own farewell to her friend, and she closed her eyes and offered one of his favorite poems as a going-away gift, spoken so softly that each syllable was muted by the patter of rain on hat brims and bowed shoulders.

"Go with God, dear friend," she added at the end, then watched woodenly as the men lowered Cal's casket on ropes. After flipping the lines clear, two cowhands with shovels began to toss the mud and rocks in on him. The dull thuds bruised her heart until it was painful to breathe, and so for a long moment she didn't.

Someone tugged at her arm and she turned to see Ritter squinting from under his hat brim, rivulets of water cascading off the edges. "Come on, it's done. You're soaked. Why don't you just go back to the house and stay there today? Another day won't hurt, and this don't look like it'll let up anytime soon. Only a fool'd go out on any kind of business in this weather. The colonel and his men'll stay in today, you can bet your bottom dollar."

She shook her arm free. "Don't be ridiculous. Since when does a little weather keep hands from working? There're chores to do and a ranch to run. Part of that is seeing to its safety. I'll be riding out as soon as I can get saddled."

Ritter shook his head and stomped off, leaving her to trail along behind. Stubborn woman, hell, he'd never seen the like. Now he supposed he'd have to tag after her, see she kept safe. Yancey Barton would skin him alive if he didn't. Well, so much for staying by the fire and trading lies with the hands. She was worse to work for than any man. Still and all, he sure did admire her.

Inside the shelter of the new barn Charlie heaved a saddle on her favorite roan Belle, tightened the cinch, and lowered the stirrup. Ritter came from the corral leading an iron-gray gelding that stood at least sixteen hands high. The mount's wide back was steaming and darkly splotched with rain. The pungent aroma of horseflesh mixed with that of the green pine smell of logs in the newly built structure.

She glared at the young hand with a baleful eye. "Where the thunder do you think you're going?"

"With you."

"Nope, you're not. There's plenty to do around this place, and you know that well."

"Dang it all, Miss Houston, I might as well ride out for Texas if I let you leave here alone. Barton'll horsewhip me."

She stepped into the stirrup and swung her right leg over the saddle. "He'll do no such thing. I still run this ranch, not Yancey Barton. He's not my daddy. He's not..." She gazed a moment at the young man through a sudden gush of tears that blurred her vision. Then grief hit her like a blast of north wind off the prairie, so hard that she swayed in the saddle. First her beloved father, now Cal. Who would be next? What payment did this vicious land demand before it gave in to be tamed?

"Oh, Ritter. Dammit," she said, and slipped from the roan's back. Her wobbly knees gave way and would have dumped her to the ground had the young man not been handy. He scooped her into his arms and carried her through the driving rain toward the house. All strength drained from her, and she allowed his action without comment.

For a long while after Ritter left, closing the door softly and silently, Charlie lay on the bed where he had placed her, his face red with embarrassment. Then she rose, woodenly removed her muddy boots that had left two big wet brown spots on the quilt, and brewed herself a cup of tea. A small fire crackled in the stove and she tossed in a few sticks from the woodpile against the wall before sitting down at the table to sip at the fragrant brew.

Memories of Cal washed over her. The way he used to scribble his poems on brown wrapping paper from the mercantile, hand them over to her so she could put music to the words. And then she would sing the tune for him until he had it memorized.

"Oh, Cal, dearest, how I'll miss that."

She finished the tea and leaving the cup on the table went to the bed and pulled out the music box. Winding it, she inserted a metal disk and snicked the lever. Chopin's Etude in E Major filled the room, and she closed her eyes, tears squeezing out from between the lids.

Bright, warm light struck the side of her face and she blinked into long rays of sunlight that had broken through the heavy clouds. Peering out the window she saw that the sun hung on the rim of the mountains to the west in a wide slat of blue sky.

Near sunset already. How had it gotten so late? Her reveries had put her in another world so that the dreary afternoon passed without her noticing it.

She gazed in silence as the orange ball slipped behind the purple peaks. Bright silver linings flared along the edges of a spatter of rain clouds. Shades of lavender, pink, and gold frosted their bilious bellies and darkness crawled across the prairie. Frogs set up a chorus of song and an owl called to a distant echo.

The cabin felt small and empty, and much too lonely. She opened the back door and leaned against the frame breathing in the cool clean night air. Moisture hung in spirals of fog, making Charlie think of one of the sonnets Cal had written about warm rains and riding trail. And how cowpokes living out under the wide, dark sky had a true appreciation for living that no one else could even imagine.

She had to get out, go somewhere where she could recapture that feeling, maybe sing a farewell to Cal.

Once it got dark Mitch circled a good distance from the ranch itself and doubled back to the ridge above the scattered buildings. He'd holed up during the rain and hadn't gone near the funeral. Anger over what had happened dwelt in him like a confined beast, eager to escape and wreak havoc. His supper of deer jerky grew thin so that his stomach growled an empty protest. He longed to sit at a table and tuck into a steaming plate of stew, chase it down with hot black coffee. He dismounted there on the ridge, his thoughts roaming like stray ponies, and dropped Jeb's reins to the ground.

Below in the cabin a figure passed by the lighted window.

He had to stop lurking around watching her like some kind of green kid. Better if he rode up and announced his intentions to lend a hand in this war with the colonel. He grinned at the thought, tried to imagine her reaction. He'd be lucky if she didn't hand him his head. And even if she didn't, she'd never believe he had changed sides. She would just think the colonel had sent him to worm his way into the enemy camp.

Approaching her had seemed the thing to do after last night. He wanted to be the one she called upon, wanted to stand beside her and fight for her dream.

After a while she started playing that haunting, melancholy music that made him think of things best left alone. Of caressing soft, dew-moist flesh, of loving a woman who loves you back, of happy times long past.

To get under his skin even more she began to sing to the music that floated in the black stillness. Amazing how sound carried in these high meadows.

The moon had yet to rise, but the night was far from dark. Some nights out here were like that, and others were like someone had dropped a black velvety blanket over everything. It was the clouds, he reckoned, for they skittered across the sky dragging stars in their wake.

At first it wasn't Charlie he watched, but a furtive figure sneaking from the back of the bunkhouse. He couldn't make out who it was, but the sneaky critter was real careful not to be seen by the guards and was soon hightailing it on foot for a stand of pines just below where Mitch stood watch.

Going careful, Mitch sneaked in for a closer look and was scarcely in place behind a boulder before the sound of a walking horse disturbed him. The mysterious rider reined up and dismounted before he came into Mitch's sight, and then walked directly to where the other man waited.

Mitch dared go no closer, and he could only hear the murmur of their voices. Someone from the Houston ranch was up to no good, it would seem.

After several minutes of quiet conversation, the man who had ridden in led his horse away from the rendezvous and passed so close by Mitch on his way out that he couldn't help but see the silver belt buckle gleaming. He'd seen a buckle like that on only one man in these parts; the gunslinger Cross that the colonel had hired only days before. The same man Mitch was pretty sure had a hand in the killing of Cal Malone.

Now who from the Houston ranch would be fool enough to meet with this killer? Somebody making a deal? But what would they have to gain? The answer of course was money, pure and simple. The colonel had someone working inside, feeding him information, and he was paying him to do so.

But who? Not the foreman Yancey Barton, surely. And probably not that young wrangler. He was so crazy about the Houston woman he followed her around like a puppy dog with his tongue hanging down to the ground. Course that left quite a few men to choose from. He could tell enough about the man to know him if he saw him again.

Mitch was so deep in thought that he didn't see him leave, only realized he was gone when he heard someone else coming and peered out to see Charlie Houston picking her way along the path. Christ, what was this? A Saturday night barn dance?

Mitch stayed right where he was. He hoped the stallion didn't take it into his head to come looking for him. He should have tied him instead of just dropping the reins like that. But Jeb didn't take to being tied and sometimes tore up Ned getting loose.

He grinned. He'd do the same, he reckoned.

Charlie Houston meandered into the clearing, capturing his attention once again. Was that all she had to do, wander around in the middle of the night? And suppose that idiot Cross doubled back and saw her, decided to have himself a little fun.

He lost sight of her for a moment as she picked her way around an outcropping of sprawling juniper brush and melted into the deep shadows. Then he heard her singing in a clear and exquisite voice that seemed to come from a stand of spruce off to his left. He stepped cautiously into the heavy darkness beneath several of the giants, but despite his care dry pine needles crunched under his boots. Abruptly the song cut off. He could almost feel her listening and he remained still for a long time, until the muscles in his legs began to quiver from the stiff position. At last she started to hum, then went back to the ballad about some trail hand pining for his lost love and finding her in the stars.

He listened until she finished, afraid to approach her but unwilling to leave her there alone. Didn't she have good sense? Out here making so damned much noise that anyone passing by would know right where she was?

Charlie stopped singing and wiped tears from her cheeks with the backs of both hands. Too much dying, too many tears. She sighed and rose from where she had perched on a boulder. As she turned to head back for the cabin, she caught a glimpse of someone darting between tree trunks just at the periphery of her vision. Quickly she judged the distance between her escape route back to the cabin and the threat. Perhaps it was one of her own men, circling the ranch on foot.

More than a little miffed, she stopped and shouted out. "Who is that? Ritter, is that you lollygagging after me again? Answer me now, you're scaring me. Come out and show yourself."

Mitch stepped from the darkness into the clearing. He could have remained hidden, but if he had she'd probably have kept hollering till the noise brought her guards. Then he might have gotten shot or been forced to shoot someone. It was better to show himself only to her.

He took off his hat and she recognized him immediately from the flare of white in his hair, as he'd hoped she would. The recognition didn't gain him the silent acceptance he'd counted on, though. Instead she called out his name in a wild, unsettling way, whirled, and ran directly into a massive clump of brush that completely entangled her. She yelped and fought, and that only got her in more trouble.

He was beside her immediately, grabbing at her. "Stop, stop struggling. You're only making it worse."

"Take your hands off me. Back away. What are you doing

out here sneaking around? Ouch, dammit." A thorn ripped at her arm and she cried out. The more she struggled the more caught up she became.

"It's gooseberries. If you don't hold still they'll rip you to pieces." His hands fumbled at working her clothing loose from the vicious thorns.

Despite the gunslinger looming over her, Charlie stopped lunging about. Both sleeves of the flannel shirt were enmeshed, a vine clung tightly to the fabric across her breasts, more wrapped around her buttocks and thighs. Every movement brought sharp, biting pain somewhere else on her body, and she panted from the struggle.

"That's better." His voice hummed in her ear he stood so close. His fingers traced the vine across her breasts, knuckles brushing at her taut nipples.

She sucked in a breath, but remained very still. "Why do you keep bothering me?"

"I could stop, but then you'd be sort of caught up in things." He grunted and plucked away a thorn, feeling for another with fingers that trailed gently over her body.

A shiver darted through her stomach down low, and she caught her lower lip in her teeth. Much as the thorns hurt, his touch upset her equilibrium even more. The teasing tone of his voice surprised her too, for he didn't seem the sort. His nature was more harsh, uncaring, cold, or so she had thought.

His touch moved from one breast to the other and sent unwanted and thoroughly unexpected waves of longing straight to her core.

He felt the trembling shudder and mistook it. "Sorry, I know it hurts like hell. Almost through." He leaned down to get a better look at his work in the darkness and his hair brushed at her chin.

She sucked in a light breath. "Oh, dear goodness."

He stopped for a moment, leaving his hand where it was, the fingers lying ever so gently against her rapidly rising and falling breast.

"Please, take your hand away." Meant to be a command, the request came out delicately and not at all demanding.

He raised his head so that their mouths were on the same level, practically breathing each other's air. "Sorry. Am I hurting you?" It was a whisper, vague and raspy, like it wasn't what he really meant to say at all.

No answer would come to her, for the thorns that remained buried in her flesh didn't cause near as much discomfort as did the desire that exploded in her. She had only to move a scant inch and their lips would touch, and she did, disregarding a thorn that plucked at her arm.

Their mouths brushed for a split second so heady Mitch forgot what he was doing and leaned closer for a better taste. The shift put tension on the branch of thorns that had wrapped itself around her right arm and they dug in unmercifully.

She moaned, as much from the lost chance as the pain, and he went back to work with renewed concentration. At last he had the front of her shirt freed and went to work on the sleeve.

"One thing at a time," he muttered.

"What?" she asked.

"Never mind. There, okay, now turn this way." His voice trembled, but he managed to get a hold on himself to go to work on the length of a vine stuck firmly across her butt.

"How'd you get yourself in such a mess anyway?"

"Well, I didn't exactly do it to myself. If you hadn't come lunging up out of the dark like some night creature I wouldn't have run in the first place." She wiggled tighter against him when he reached around her.

"Hmmm," he said, and circled her waist with his other arm to hold her tight.

"What are you doing?"

"You don't know what I'm doing? It seems we've been at this long enough for you to have figured it out."

"Well, don't hug me so tight."

"Have to if I'm going to... there, I think you're free." His voice sounded gruff and angry all of a sudden.

She lurched to get out of his reach only to find that one pant leg was still held firmly in the grasp of a thorny branch.

He clasped her once again around the waist. "Hold it, you're just going to make it worse. We're almost there."

"I can get loose myself now, if you'd just let go."

He did and stepped back. "Fine by me." The anger was definitely there now.

The hat he'd crammed back on his head kept her from seeing his face, even though her night vision let her make out his size and shape pretty well. She bent over to untangle her leg and a row of thorns planted themselves firmly across her buttocks, sticking deep into the jeans fabric to bite at her skin once again. She tried to jerk away and raked the back of her hand over another cluster of the vicious thorns.

Crying out as much in frustration as pain, she gave up and stood there trapped.

He did nothing.

"Well?" she said.

"What?"

"Help me."

"Oh. I thought you said—"

"Help me is what I said."

"Sounds like an order to me."

She sighed and pretended ignorance. "And you don't take

orders except from our illustrious colonel. Look, I'd appreciate it if you would give me a hand here."

"I'd be pleased, Miss Houston, to give you a hand if you'll stop squirming and shouting like some sissy female."

"I am not… never mind, never mind. Go away entirely if you wish, leave me hanging out here till some wolf comes along and makes a meal out of me. That'd be more to your way of doing things, wouldn't it, Mr. Fallon? And just what are you doing out here anyway? Ouch, dammit!"

"You said that already," he said. "You ready to hold still, or do you have more to say? I'm here trying to save your… uh… well, your skin, and all you want to do is criticize. I haven't even heard a thank you, not one."

"Thank you? Thank you? I have no more to say," she replied, and tightened her lips together. If and when he ever got her loose from here, she would take great pleasure in smacking him good. She would double up her fist and hit him right in the mouth, see how he liked that, the smart-ass. But first, let him untangle her from this mess.

"Well, that's better. Being polite never hurt anyone."

She took a deep breath and closed her eyes.

Damn smarty pants.

His hands worked all over her backside, loosening one thorn at a time. Leaning this way and that his body brushed up against hers, muscles lean and hard and enticing, and she was certain he was doing it on purpose.

When he shifted to one side to free the final thorn from her backside the slant of his jaw touched her ear and a puff of his breath stirred her hair. She shivered. He smelled like camp smoke and the deep woods, a whiff of leathery saddle mixed in, and his touch was definitely doing things to her she hadn't expected, especially under such extreme circumstances. She was furious with the man, scared of what had happened, suspicious of what he was doing out here so close to her home, and yet the gentle touch of his fingers, the patient way he went about extricating her from the thorns made her anything but frightened.

He kept uttering little syllables that weren't really words but were meant to be reassuring. Then she felt his hand under her arm so that the palm and thumb cupped the swell of her breast. An amazed "Ohhh" escaped her lips.

"Sorry," he murmured. "Dammit, if you'd hold still."

She squeezed her eyes shut. "I would if you'd stop... if you'd stop." But she didn't want him to stop touching her, even disregarding the circumstances. She held very still, for the thorns had gouged deeply into the very tenderest of her flesh and the wounds were beginning to hurt badly. Tears ran from under her closed lids.

For an instant he stopped moving. "Don't cry."

"I'm not."

"Your tears are falling on my hands," he said very softly.

She sniffed, bit her lip. Deep down in her belly, where the fiery caress of the gooseberry thorns could not go, a longing stirred like coals fanned by a night wind. This man, this frightening man who seemed so gentle and so harsh all at the same time, threatened her sensibilities like none ever had.

He wanted to gather her up in his arms and tell her it was okay to cry when she hurt. He suspected all the pain wasn't coming from the thorns by the way she'd been singing so sadly earlier. He cupped her buttocks and pulled her gently toward him and away from the damaging bushes. She came close to him without objection. Her firm, soft breasts pressed against him. He drew in a deep breath and held her for a moment, forgetting the task at hand.

Dear God in heaven, if he didn't turn her loose soon he'd

make a complete fool of himself. He wanted to kiss her not pry thorns out of her behind.

"What are you doing?" she asked, but he heard no reprimand in her tone.

Without answering he remained pressed against her, both arms holding her in a firm embrace. He closed his eyes and took a very deep breath, then stepped back. Letting her go left a hollow spot near his heart that ached with emptiness.

"Okay, if you don't start flailing around again, you'll be free at last." He spoke in a deliberately harsh tone. Damn her anyway, butting her way into his life when he'd had it all figured out.

Despite the tone, she didn't reply or offer to battle with him over his attitude. Her lack of fight caused him to feel sorry for her. A woman like her, put more or less at someone's mercy, must be awful uneasy. She was probably itching to lash out because of all the evil deeds she thought he'd committed. About some of them, she was right, but how could he convince her that he wasn't her enemy? And what the hell did he care, anyway? Caring was a good way to get a quick kick in the teeth. He wanted no part of that kind of pain, ever again.

With a tight grip on her upper arm he led her carefully out of reach of the wicked gooseberry bushes, then dropped his hands away as if they'd been burned.

She stood there for a long moment, regarding the hulking shadow whose face she already knew well even though she couldn't make it out. She rubbed at the fire burning her flesh, caused as much by his proximity as the long scratches dug by the thorns.

"You're fine now," he said hoarsely.

"Thank you." She began to shiver violently. "Please, I... I want to go to the house."

"I'll take you," he said, and grabbed her arm and began

to drag her out of the shadows and into the open. There was no question of breaking away from the iron-hard grip. She just stumbled along beside him.

The moon peeked through racing clouds and illuminated everything: the umber dark trees, the stretch of meadow laced in pale ivory, a black horse that moved up on them seemingly from out of nowhere.

She stumbled again, tugged at his shirt. "Please slow down. What are you so mad about?"

He stopped and turned toward her. In that moment lowered his head to look down at her, she thought she saw moisture gleaming in his eyes. But surely not. She dismissed the idea.

"What are you doing out here alone in the middle of the damned night anyway? Is that all you've got to do? Traipse around in the middle of the night taking baths and causing Indian uprisings and getting yourself all caught up in thorns?" In one swift motion he swung her up in his arms and resumed the long stride, carrying her along easy as could be.

In her head she shouted at him to put her down, that she could walk by herself, but in the depths of her soul she embraced his warmth, his strength, his solidity. The beating of his heart in her ear, the male aroma, the touch of skin where his shirt parted down his chest, eased the pain buried so deeply within her.

There was no place to put her arms except around his neck where the softness of his hair whispered over her flesh.

He spoke no further, but kept right on walking. The black horse followed, his head nodding up and down right beside her feet. Neither master nor beast appeared to pay her any mind at all.

When he had deposited her at the back door from which she'd exited earlier, he broke the silence gruffly, "There, home without harm. Well, at least without much. You'd better put something on those scratches or they'll be sore in the morning. Good night, Miss Houston, and you're welcome."

"Fine, sir. And I'd like you to stop...stop following me around." The lie tumbled out weakly, both of them knowing she didn't mean it at all.

Without honoring her with even a grunt for a reply, he mounted the horse with agile grace and rode away.

Nine

She slept in the arms of her lover, and awoke once in the middle of the night wondering who she was and where she lay, but his lips were at her breast there in that dream, and so she drifted back to him on mounds of pink clouds.

He held her in exquisite passion, one hand cupped between her thighs, lips tasting the sweet bud of each breast as if it were coated in honey.

She did not know who he was, perhaps he had no face, for he would not turn it to her, but kept it pressed to her flesh so all she could see was a fan of black hair spread over her like a dark angel's robe. There was a streak of pure white running through it. She wrapped her legs around his waist and he rose from their downy bed taking her with him into the ebony sky where he made love to her until dawn and then was gone, leaving her to caress only silver beams of light.

She awoke to an empty bed crying huge tears that splotched her pillow.

The dream, though a vast improvement over nightmares of stampedes and death, left an unsettling longing she couldn't fulfill. She found herself wishing Mitchell Fallon would come through the door and finish what he had started when he carried her from the tangle of gooseberry vines.

To make matters worse, and despite the star-studded night, a dreary rain moved once more over the valley the next morning. Once she dressed and had breakfast, two leftover biscuits from the night before, she left the cabin and its lingering dream images and went to the barn. Today she would not be dissuaded from riding the range, and the ensuing argument with Ritter echoed much the same conversation they had carried on the day before when she had given way to her grief and let him win.

It would not happen this time, for she had to be on the move, not closed up in the cabin with desires she didn't understand and couldn't consummate.

When Ritter finally glared at her in helpless disgust, his every objection shot down, she took some pity on him.

"Don't trouble yourself about what Yancey will do to you. I give the orders around here, no matter what he and you might like to think. You'll stay here and mend tack, it's in horrible shape. And when that's done, there's stove wood to chop. And Crane could use some more firewood too, while you're at it.

"I'll ride the circuit, just like I told you. Yancey comes in, you tell him so." She stepped lithely into the saddle, tugged the roan's head around, and urged it forward into the dismal weather.

"Fool woman. I'm a blamed cowboy, not a greenhorn jingler." Ritter continued to mutter under his breath and turned to fiddle with the gray gelding's bit. "Her orders is everyone rides out in pairs, but she rides out alone pretty as you please. Can't blame me if she's scalped or hung for a rustler or gunned down by the colonel's men."

There would be hell to pay no matter what he did, and Ritter knew it. He figured the choice he had to make was to look out for her, so he remained back in the darkness of the barn until the thick soup of mist, fog, and rain swallowed up her lone figure, then he mounted and urged the gelding to follow.

Sometime later a third rider joined the bedraggled parade. Mitch Fallon had spent the night in his camp under the thick stand of spruce, and kicked his heels into the stallion's sides soon after Charlie plodded past him. He heard the second rider coming, the footfalls muted on the saturated ground, and retreated into the shadows to wait for his passage. It was that young boy everyone called Ritter. The one that dogged her every step. Mitch recognized the overgrown Montana Stetson that nestled low over his forehead. She had her a guard of sorts, and he admired the young man for his bulldog determination. The woman would probably hogtie him to a tree if she caught him following her. Mitch feared Ritter would not be able to protect her from the likes of a killer like Cross, though. When the huge gray horse and its diminutive rider disappeared into the murkiness, Mitch fell in at the rear of the procession. If she caught him she'd tie him up with the same rope as she used on Ritter, but it couldn't be helped.

After what Cross and Neddy had done to Cal Malone, and then the gunman's midnight rendezvous with one of her hands last night, Mitch wasn't taking any chances that the pretty owner of the Double H might be the next target

Odd how he felt about her, and with no stake in this whatsoever, he still couldn't just ride away. That had all been settled the night before when he'd untangled her and then carried her to the cabin. Their lips and their bodies had touched, her tears had fallen on his flesh, and he had looked into her soul. It had taken every ounce of willpower he had to ride off and leave her at the door. What he had wanted to do was follow her inside and fold up around her on the bed, hold her close all night. Immerse himself in her bouquet of leather-scented sweetness, breathe the very air she did, caress her delicate wildness. Find out who she was, really. Explore the being that lay hidden deep down inside her. Maybe even show her his true self if she cared to look.

The fiery ranch owner had wormed her way into his life, and he couldn't dig her out with a spade. Maybe, just maybe, he didn't want to, even though thinking about the sheer impossibility of it tended to make him mad. There was certainly no percentage in sticking up for the underdog, he'd learned that a long time ago, yet he could do nothing else. It was much too late. He should never have laid a hand on her, nor gotten close enough to exchange breaths, to look into those cavernous eyes, to brush lips with her. God almighty.

Charlie paused several times to get her bearings in the gloom, other than that she kept moving at a pretty steady pace. Once she heard the harsh cough of a cow and realized she had ridden into a herd of grazing longhorns in the low-hanging mist. Each in turn raised a head, balefully regarding the intruder while they chewed the sweet green grass.

In spite of the poncho and wide-brimmed hat, she was soon wet clear through. Cold seeped into every pore so that she shivered. Better put up at Cal's ranch for the night and get a fresh start in the morning.

She expected no one to be at the ranch. There hadn't been time for Zeke to file a claim in Virginia City and return, yet a saddled pony stood hipshot at the hitching rail out front.

Surprised and a little cautious, she drew closer and saw that the saddle and bedroll were soaked as was the poor animal. His head drooped and rain drizzled from his velvety chin. The cow pony carried the Rocking R brand, and she recognized it as one Zeke was fond of riding. How had it gotten here? Maybe Zeke rode another mount. That still didn't explain this one.

Something was very wrong. No cowpuncher leaves his horse standing out in the rain until it's this wet, not with a barn so near. The black window openings of the small ranch house stared balefully at her. Empty places exuded a peculiar sense of abandonment, this one even more so, and she could almost hear Cal's ghost warning her to beware. With all that had happened recently, she feared dismounting and walking up on the place without taking a few precautions.

Her heart slammed into her throat as she imagined someone inside taking a bead on her, and she remained mounted thinking about what this could mean. Something had to have happened to this poor horse's rider. Something dreadful.

At last she swallowed hard and dismounted. Her heart wouldn't stop its thumping, and for good measure she took the Winchester out of its scabbard and jacked a shell into the chamber. Tying Belle beside the bedraggled cow pony, she crept as quietly as possible up the path to the porch. On her toes she went up the steps and slipped along the front of the house to a window to peek inside. Raindrops pecked incessantly on the roof and dripped onto the saturated ground, the only sound but for her own breathing and the thundering of her heart.

Easing to the door she reached out with one gloved hand to push it open. It creaked and she hunched her shoulders, waiting and holding her breath. Not the slightest movement or sound issued from inside. That was worse than a noise.

"Zeke?" she whispered through the open door. "Zeke? You in there?"

Foolish thing to ask. There was no reply, and she gingerly put a toe against the door to swing it open farther. Inside something ran across the floor, squealing and making a terrible clatter. A shout escaped from between her clenched lips and she jumped backward, almost toppling off the porch.

"Holy cow," a man hollered from out of the mist at her back. "What the tarnation's going on, Miss Houston?"

Hands clutching at her throat, Charlie whirled. "Ritter, what are you doing here?"

The young cowboy vaulted from the tall gelding and double-timed it to her side. "What's going on? What happened?"

"Ritter, I thought I… never mind. Look, it's Zeke's horse, and he's been here a long time. Oh, Ritter, what do you suppose has happened?"

"You stay here. I'm just fixing to find out." He started to go in the door, then turned and pointed at her. "And I mean it, if you'll excuse me. Stay put!"

In this case, she was only too glad to obey.

Ritter shoved at the door, but something was holding it and he had to lay a shoulder into it hard to force the thing open enough to squeeze inside.

Zeke lay crumpled on the floor, blood drying around him in a great wide pool. His head was cocked back at a crazy angle and what Ritter could see of his face was covered in blood as well. He took hold of the dead man's shoulder and rolled him away from the door. When the body came to rest Ritter saw that Zeke had been scalped.

Foul-tasting bile poured into his mouth and he made a fist over his lips. He stayed hunkered there for a moment until his belly quit heaving, then he stood and removed his hat. Dirty savage Indians. As if they didn't already have enough trouble with the colonel and his rampaging, now they had the Cheyenne on the warpath. He knew some families of Northern Cheyenne were camped out over toward the Bighorn River, Indians who thought nothing of venturing into range land to cut out a few cattle once in a while. A couple of them had even had the nerve to beg some beeves off Miss Charlie. Some of the hands had reported sightings of Sioux lately, renegades off the reservation in Dakota Territory.

"Ritter, what is it?" Charlie called from outside. "Ritter, please, answer me."

Before he could reply he heard approaching hoofbeats and a man's voice. "Miss Houston, you okay? What in the hell's going on here?"

"Fallon! What is this, a camp meeting? Ritter, if you don't come out this instant, I'm coming in, orders or no."

"On my way," Ritter said, and his voice broke crazily so that he had to swallow and try again. "I'm coming out now."

He stepped onto the porch to see a tall man dressed in black striding forcefully up the walk, one large hand resting menacingly on the butt of a Colt .44 in a low-slung holster.

Ritter grabbed her arm and yelled, "Dammit, run, Miss Houston, that's one of the colonel's men."

She shook off the young man and swung around so that the barrel of her rifle pointed toward the intruder even though she held it loosely at her side. She regarded Fallon with cool disdain, not at all like the inner turmoil she felt.

Ritter darted a glance from one to the other. If he'd been armed, he would have drawn down on the scoundrel and shot him on the spot, but Miss Charlie just stood there with her Winchester dangling.

The gunman mounted the steps and ignored Ritter to question Miss Charlie. "Are you hurt? Who's in there?"

"Of course I'm not hurt, and I don't know yet. Let's ask Ritter, shall we?" She turned and gave Ritter such a look that he cringed.

He hated to tell her about Zeke, but more than that he dreaded her wrath. It would all probably be directed at him, and he'd had nothing to do with Zeke's death. And why was she taking the appearance of the gunslinger so casually?

Miss Charlie and the stranger glared at him as if he had

something to do with Zeke lying dead in there. He gulped, unable to say anything.

"I'll just go see for myself." She started to push past him.

Ritter grabbed her arm. "No, no don't." He appealed to the gunman, not sure whose side he was on, but then the man took her other arm.

"It's probably best you don't go in there," he told her softly. "What is it, boy?"

"It... it's Zeke, Mr. Cal's foreman. He's been... he's been *scalped*." Ritter shivered uncontrollably and ran off the porch to upchuck in the bushes. He felt more than a little miserable, and wished he were back in the bunkhouse wrapped in blankets instead of standing wet in the rain and puking.

Charlie ignored poor Ritter. "Oh, dear God, dear God, no. What's happening? Why would they do this?" She tried to envision savage Indians, knives at the ready hacking away at the bloody scalp, but all she could think of were the soft brown eyes of Spotted Moon's wife, the child sleeping in her arms. This would mean trouble for the Indians, for sure. And the women and children would suffer the most.

She stumbled as if dizzy or disoriented, and Mitch wrapped his arms around her. Her breath came hot through his shirt and little tremors passed from her to him. He wanted to gather her up and carry her away to a warm, dry place where he could soothe her grief. He could think of nothing to say, so he patted at the back of her head and leaned his cheek down into the tangle of dark hair.

Dear God, he'd forgotten how good it felt to hold a woman in his arms. How soft and sweet they were. How completely helpless they could be.

"You probably did this." She hauled off and kicked him in the shin.

He let out a surprised "Ow" and stumbled away from her.

Whirling, she tried to push past and go inside the house.

Ritter grabbed her. "No, Miss Charlie, don't go in there. He didn't do it." He gestured toward the gun-fighter. "You don't want to go in there. It was Indians, I promise you."

Fire in her eyes, she pointed a trembling finger at the cow pony still tied to the hitching rail. "When did you ever see an Indian leave a perfectly good horse behind? White men did this, and you can bet they're tied in with the colonel."

She was nearly sputtering with fury when she darted her gaze toward Fallon. Somehow, he was to blame for this. She just knew it. How could she have let him put his hands all over her the other night? How could he be so helpful and soft-spoken knowing what horrible thing lay in there?

"You'll do anything, won't you? Anything. How can a man like you live with himself? Well, you didn't have to kill Zeke. He was no threat to anyone, he just wanted to stay in the saddle and do his job. An honest man, he was an honest man, just like Cal."

She tilted her head to look up into his face, shout, "When are you going to kill me?"

He studied her intently, absorbing the hate that emanated from her like heat boiling from a prairie fire. He didn't blame her much, but he wished she didn't feel this way about him. He'd observed her in her most private moments when she thought she was alone. He'd held her nearly naked body in his arms, he'd picked thorns from that sweet flesh. What could be more intimate? He felt as if his soul was completely lost to her. There had to be a way he could make her believe that all he wanted was for her to be safe.

She had grown ominously silent, standing rigid with one hand clenched around that rifle and her shoulders thrown back. Though tears continued to run down her cheeks, she kept her eyes on him, not flinching or backing down. If he had been the man she thought he was, he would have killed her and the foolish boy right on the spot and ridden off. But she didn't yet realize that.

Damn her for getting inside him and making him feel he owed her or any of these other fools anything. And then turn around and accuse him of the killing.

With furious control he said, "No, I didn't kill the man inside, I didn't kill your friend, and I will not kill you. No matter what you think. You and this boy get yourselves back to your ranch before something happens you can't stop."

He nodded curtly and strode across the porch, the jingles on his spurs ringing merrily in the sodden air. Shoulders hunched, he waited for the bullet she would send into his back, but none came. He would only go so far as to be out of her sight, but no farther. Whether she liked it or not, he would not leave until this was over.

Without asking permission, he untied the poor drenched cow pony, led him into the barn, and unsaddled him. Before turning him loose he rubbed him down with a gunny sack. The tough little quarter horse made snuffling sounds and nudged Mitch on the back with his nose in a gesture of thanks as he worked.

"It's okay, boy. No one deserves to be left out in the cold and wet, not even a poor old horse like you." Finished with the chore, he strode out to his own mount, climbed into the saddle, and rode off.

He didn't look back to see if she watched him leave, but he had a hunch she did, damning him every step of the way.

Charlie's teeth chattered but she remained where she was, not moving an inch while the lowering mist swallowed Fallon. Maybe she could have shot him if he'd come at her with hate and malice in his green eyes. Gunned him down for the monster he was, but not this way, not a back shot. Those eyes had transmitted nothing of a killer. Sorrow perhaps, melancholy, confusion even, but no threat.

"I was going to stay here the night," she then told Ritter in a sad voice.

"Well, you can. I'll just move the body. I can put him in the barn." He was eager to please, do anything to help her, she looked so forlorn and lost with her hair all smashed down by wearing the hat in the rain all day and her skin gray with shock.

"Oh, no. No. I couldn't stay in there now. Not with...." She broke off and waved a limp hand toward the open door.

"Well, the barn then. It'll be dry in there and you'll be fine. I'll keep watch."

She reached out and touched his arm. "Thank you, Ritter. You're very nice, even though you do trail around behind me like some hound." Glancing around quickly, she went on. "You know I'd rather the Indians had done this than those awful men who work for the colonel. At least they have a reason for killing white men. Reckon he...I mean, he got here awful quick. Could have been just hanging around after... you know." Her head nodded in the direction in which Fallon had ridden off.

"Well, maybe, I don't know. I just can't figure a white man doing something like that, but then a man will do some pretty awful things sometimes."

"What are we going to do...I mean, with the body?"

He raised his shoulders. "Maybe I ought to bury him. I could put him up on the hill with Mr. Cal." He arched his neck and stared up into the heavy clouds. "This looks like it ain't gonna quit very soon, and I hate to think of him just laying in there like that."

"Well, I guess that's best. I'll give you a hand."

She took a deep breath, dragging in the clean wet air that

tasted of pine and mountain snows. She was through crying, it was a weak and feminine thing to do, and like Ritter had once said, she didn't do womanly things. Before he could stop her, she jumped off the porch and ran to the barn, forgetting that her hat was still lying where it had fallen when Mitch Fallon wrapped her in his arms. Thinking of that, she felt hot all over. For just a moment, when Fallon had pulled her to his chest and laid his cheek against her hair, she'd almost lost all sense and forgotten who the man was.

Every time they got together he did something for her.

Hair dripping she ran inside the barn and began looking for a shovel to dig Zeke's grave.

When the bolt of lightning struck later that night she was dreaming about the stampede that had killed her father. With tight fists she knuckled away the nightmare vision of St. Elmo's fire crackling across the horns of the charging cattle herd that had trampled him. Even after she came awake, the smell of burning hair lingered.

Despite the storm, the air in the barn was warm, and she could smell the steam off the horses, hear them breathing and snuffling in sleep.

The lightning strike appeared to signal the passing of the storm, for the rain on the roof let up and the intermittent flashes of light and rumbling thunder faded into the distance.

She sat in the hay for a moment, stretching her aching muscles, then crept through the velvety darkness to the door. A heavy bar held it shut, and she hoisted it, careful not to make any noise that would awaken Ritter. As the door swung inward she saw fire licking into the sky, throwing a crimson reflection onto the low scudding clouds. For a moment she was terrified, then as she stepped out into the rainwashed night, she realized that a huge Ponderosa pine had been split in half. The enormous jagged trunk left standing shot fire high into the sky. The heat from the flames touched her face and lit up the barnyard. Eerie shadows played with orange reflections in puddles of rain.

She felt strangely removed from reality, as if she walked within the confines of a dream in which she could do anything she wished without consequence. And indeed, perhaps she was still lying asleep in the hay.

He emerged from the shadows, appeared to simply materialize out of the intense blaze that leaped and danced at his back, and she fought an intense desire to go to him. He wore no hat or shirt. A gust of wind lifted his hair, whipping the white streak upward as if to join the flames.

Mesmerized, she waited for him to come to her. There was no fear in her, even though she thought there should be. She watched with amazement as her trembling fingers reached out to him. His eyes shot tiny flecks of red and yellow and he reached out a hand to meet hers, fingertips touching fingertips. She gazed into his face until a dark shadow fell over it when he came away from the firelight. This man with such acute sadness in his eyes quivered as he touched her.

Without hesitation she moved closer, into the emanating heat he'd absorbed from the fire. It washed through the cool air between them, encompassing her. He lifted her hand toward his mouth. She thought he would kiss it, but instead he placed her knuckles along his jaw and held them there.

She swayed, closed her eyes a moment. Dear God, she was so very tired of being alone.

He put his arms around her, gently at first, then enfolding her in an eager lover's embrace. Her fingers played through his hair, slightly damp from the rain and warm from the fire. His mouth on hers was hot and wet, the desire that shot through her as vivid as bolts of lightning left from the storm.

Groaning, he lifted her off her feet, held her so close she could feel the laddering of his ribs, the rise and fall of his breathing.

Perhaps she was indeed imagining it all, lying in the barn dreaming, but for the moment it was real. For that brief, ecstatic moment, she clung to a man who had come to her from a bolt of lightning, and she wanted nothing more in life than to be with him, experience in all its glory the extraordinarily keen sense of gratification. The world could have disappeared and she wouldn't have cared one bit at that moment. The ache in her heart eased at his touch and she wanted it all. Everything he had to offer, all he ever had been and ever was.

"Charlie Houston," he whispered into her mouth, his tongue lapping the velvety softness of her under lip.

He lowered her back to her feet then, took away his arms, and stepped backward. She blinked, cupped her face in both hands, leaned down, and with a feathery touch brushed her lips with his, then pulled away so quickly she had no time to react.

She said nothing, but only because she was dumbstruck to find him gone as if in a pouf of dust-devil cloud, leaving her to stare at the destructive fire that rose like a pillar of flame into heaven. It might well have swallowed him up, for all she knew. His departure left her feeling as if she'd lost something, and she stood there for a long time, tongue licking at his taste, a faint pungency that reminded her of new grass drenched in early morning dew.

The anger came almost as an afterthought, and she wasn't sure who to aim it at. The man who had entered her life like a dark angel to steal her soul, or herself, for being so dim-witted as to let a gunslinger kiss her. Had she gone mad?

She turned her back on the crackling fire and raced into the barn, her looming shadow dancing hugely in front of her like an uncanny companion trying to warn her of some dire destiny she had not yet dreamed of herself.

Ten

With the barn door closed at her back, Charlie remained very still, allowing the darkness to soak up the pounding of her heart. Ritter snored softly, a small animal skittered into the far corner, and her heart continued to thump wildly in her ears. She wondered if it would ever slow down again.

A desire to lie with this dark devil of a man, feel his mouth caress her most sensitive, secret places, overpowered her. She would open herself to his need, his manly, exquisite, frightful desires. She shook her head so hard lights flashed behind her lids.

"Stop this, stop it now! This is not a man you can trust. Foolish, foolish woman. Wake up."

She remained still until her eyes grew accustomed to the inky blackness inside the barn, then made her way back to the bedroll. Instead of sleeping, she greeted the man in black who returned to haunt her.

Gently she moved the tips of her fingers along the ridged scar above his eye, opened her mouth eagerly to his, tasted the flavor and felt the texture of his sensuous lips. So real, so like life that she shivered and slipped her cold hands between her thighs to warm them in the heat gathering there.

Mitch sat on the porch of the ranch house after Charlie Houston vanished into the barn. He could still feel her mouth under his, satiny smooth and slightly open in surprise. He could have had her then if he'd wanted, but hell, he didn't even know why he'd kissed her. Bedding her should be the furthest thing from his mind, yet in that storm-charged instant he'd almost swept her up and carried her inside the barn to lie with her, take her by force if need be. Some things were not meant to be taken roughly, though, and a man had to know when to use brute power and when not to.

He wished again that he had ridden off to Idaho when he had the chance, then immediately changed his mind. By now he would be in the mountains, and she would be rushing headlong toward disaster. The colonel would have what he wanted.

He gazed into the night sky a long time, thinking about that. He could stop this. And what he would have to do wouldn't be much worse than anything he'd done in the war. Celia had done her best to make a peaceful man out of him, driving away the demons. But they returned in full when he held her bloody body in his arms. Not much in his life had ever made any sense, and it seemed that each time he came close to fulfilling a desire, it was snatched away.

All he had to do was eliminate Charlie Houston's enemies. He slipped the Colt from its holster and ran a thumb over the cylinder, cocking back the hammer so it would roll freely. He could kill every one of them, these men who wouldn't stop this madness. He could do that for her, and then ride away.

Gently he let the hammer back down and sat for a long while with the gleaming pistol lying across his lap.

If he allowed his feelings to rule, he would love her and lose her, and he couldn't bear that to happen. He might have to die to protect her, and that he could do, but he couldn't watch a woman he loved die. Not again. He just couldn't. And he had a terrible suspicion that it was too late not to love her.

With trembling fingers he touched the ridged scar above his eye. In the darkness flashed memories of that dreadful day, Celia and the babe sprawled in the street in Bismarck. Throwing himself at first one, then the other of her attackers, beaten until he was bloodied and on his hands and knees. There were too many of them, and those good citizens who stood by simply watched. Groggy, dizzy, out of his mind, he gathered his dead wife and child into his arms. Covered with their blood and his, he rocked and moaned and cursed his own weakness, his inability to protect them. Only then, when he could fight no longer, had one of the men put him out of his misery, sending him into oblivion with a vicious blow from his gun. Why they hadn't killed him he never knew. But God knows, he'd prayed they had often enough.

He came to much later lying on a table in a saloon in that horrid town. A man who said he was a doctor leaned close and stitched at the wound above his eye. In the background a piano tinkled, a woman shrieked in delight.

The doctor quieted Mitch's desire to get up and put his fist through a wall or someone's face. "Hold still while I sew your head back together. Wonder they didn't kill you, son."

When Mitch struggled, cried out her name, the doctor called for help to hold him down while he finished. He wet a cloth with whiskey and cleaned around the wound that ran from his patient's eyebrow up into his scalp, then wrapped a bandage firmly around Mitch's head.

"Lay there awhile before you move around." The doctor nodded at the two men, and they let go Mitch's shoulders and glided out of his sight. He felt disoriented and weak, his vision blurry. No one paid any more attention to him, just left him draped over the table like a hunk of meat.

And how he'd railed at them all, like some kind of madman, finally struggling to his feet to stagger around in the dismal place, bumping into tables and chairs and customers until they just sort of herded him outside where he stumbled to his knees in the dusty street. No one gave a damn what happened to him.

"Where are they?" he screamed then, and raised his arms toward a distant, uncaring sky.

But he never found out what the townspeople had done with the bodies of Celia and Fawn. He didn't remember much about the next few days. He awoke one morning lying beside his horse in a ditch out in the Badlands, and didn't know how he had gotten there or what had happened. It was weeks before any of the memories came back, and when they did he wished like hell they hadn't.

Sitting there on the porch steps, he dragged his thoughts away from those awful days to think about the woman he'd held in his arms only minutes earlier. He gazed into a night sky ablaze with starlight. Cool air from the mountains chased after the passing storm and kissed his cheeks. Tomorrow would be a pretty day. Too pretty a day to die. For a good long while every day had been a perfect day to die. He examined his newfound feelings, his desire to live, and was struck dumb.

He rose, stretched both arms high above his head, and took a deep breath. Something passed from him, no stronger than a sigh, a touch of night wind, but it left behind a refreshing release from the bondage of the past.

The band of Cheyenne came just at daybreak, when silver and gold streaked the rain washed sky into a gleaming pearlescence. A tall and impressive brave led them—there were no more than a dozen, some of them very young.

Mitch had dozed propped up against the porch post, and stumbled to his feet when he heard the muffled hoofbeats. Both arms out away from his body so they could see he wasn't going for his Colt, he waited.

The Indians were painted for war, as were their horses, and his mouth grew dry. Word was that Custer and his Seventh Cavalry were in Montana to take care of the Indian problem. Once and for all, some said. There'd been a skirmish up on the Little Powder River early in the spring while snow still dusted the ground. Mitch dreaded what would eventually come of the army's plans. Would Celia's people, the mighty Sioux, at last be driven from the face of the earth forever?

He greeted the Cheyenne with cool politeness. Perhaps one of them spoke English.

His "Good morning" was considered before the Indian in the lead raised a hand and halted his pony. The rest drew up just behind him and spread out in a jagged line.

"I am Spotted Moon."

"I am Fallon."

The Indian tilted his head toward the ranch house. "We heard that this man was killed by the whites."

For a moment Mitch was confused. His thoughts were on the murdered and scalped Zeke, but immediately he realized they must be talking about Cal Malone.

"The man who owned this ranch is dead, yes," he said.

"No man owns land. Land is for The People, as far as the eye can see." Spotted Moon paused a moment to consider. "We Cheyenne, the Dakota, the Absarokas, the Crees and Shoshones, the Burned Thigh Assiniboines, the Waist and Skirt People. If we fight it is among ourselves for coup. The whites have no right to the honor of battle with The People."

Mitch nodded. "Yes, I understand."

The brave went on in his deliberate English, as if Mitch had not said anything. "Long Hair drove us from our land, and now he is coming here. Soon we will fight with *Hi-es-tzie*, but do not think he will win this last great battle. Our Chief Lame White

Man joins Crazy Horse and Sitting Bull. There will be no more white man on our lands as long as the sun rises."

Mitch knew the Cheyenne was referring to George Armstrong Custer when he spoke of Long Hair and *Hi-es-tzie*. And he dreaded what would happen. The vast tribes of the Sioux, whom this Indian referred to as the Dakota, had moved with these people from the Black Hills reservation to the Powder and Bighorn River country a couple of years back after Custer blazed the infamous Thieves Road that led to the discovery of gold in Dakota Territory. Custer had tangled with the Indians on more than one occasion, had fought with Sitting Bull twice back in '73.

Who was at fault really mattered little, for Mitch judged that the Indian would soon be destroyed. It was the only way the white man could survive. And survive he would.

But he didn't deny Spotted Moon's claim, he simply stood there regarding the proud and fearsome Cheyenne brave and waited for what would come next.

Just at that moment, the thing he had prayed wouldn't happen did. The barn door burst open and out came Charlie and Ritter.

"Spotted Moon," the woman called, and ran to the Indian at the head of the band.

"Split Skirt, it is good to see you."

"What are you doing here?" Her quick eye took in the war paint and she thought of Zeke and his hideous death. Had the Cheyenne finally decided that peace would not save them and scalped poor Zeke in there? Perhaps they had killed Cal, the braves were armed with breechloaders and magazine rifles. Though she doubted her wandering suppositions, she felt a tingle of fear standing there gazing up into the fathomless dark eyes that reflected the bravery of a mighty nation. At the same time, she was cannily aware of the presence of Fallon, though he hadn't spoken directly to her.

"You are a friend to The People," Spotted Moon said. "We wish to tell you that we will soon join together over there." He raised his arm straight and stiff and pointed across the rolling plains toward the timbered mountains of the Bighorns and the river the Indians called Greasy Grass.

"I wish you would return to the reservation, Spotted Moon."

"We cannot. They take our ponies, they take our guns, and we have nothing, and now they ravage our land. It is enough. We will fight, and you must not get hurt. Split Skirt, you have fed my people, not because you were afraid but because you have a spirit within you.

"Once I helped the white man to find his way, and he taught me to speak his words. Now I tell you that this is the last time I will allow the white man's words to roll from my tongue."

The Indian crossed his arm over his chest, fist touching the place where his heart beat, as if saluting her, then he emitted a bloodcurdling yell. The entire party replied in kind, kicking their ponies into motion.

For a long while after the braves rode out of sight Charlie stood with her hands held stiffly at her sides. Finally she said, "They will die. They will all die."

"They deserve it," Ritter muttered. "Look what they did to old Zeke. And who knows, maybe they even killed Cal. There's going to be a lot of bloodshed. Miss Charlie, I wish you would just ride back to the ranch."

While Ritter spoke, Mitch studied Charlie, awestruck by her compassion for a people she could scarcely know. She kept her eyes on the departing braves until they were nothing but a lingering cloud of dust, and he saw the sadness in her features. If she became too deeply involved in this Indian problem, then she would face more danger than she already did from Colonel Dunkirk.

He struggled to tell her so. "The Dakota are a proud people, I think they've been pushed as far as they'll push. Old Crazy Horse and Sitting Bull aren't gonna back up anymore. At some point, they're going to turn and fight. I hope that idjit Custer realizes that.

"We'll see plenty of blood shed here by the colonel and his bunch too. For that reason, Miss Houston, I think your hand here is right. You should go back to your ranch and hole up if you refuse to sell out and leave. I'm afraid the colonel is out to destroy you and all the others like you. And he's only just started."

Charlie listened to his words with a heart heavy as death. This man, her enemy, her nemesis, both attracted and frightened her. She whirled, eyes swimming in tears. "And why would you care? Your gun is paid for by the brute. For all I know you're just following me around to keep track of me for the colonel."

Mitch settled his black hat down carefully on his head. "Nope, that isn't so. Not anymore, but I don't expect you to believe that. I'll just get my horse and ride, if you'll excuse me. I quit the colonel when that animal Cross killed your friend Malone. I don't much care if you believe me or not, but I do wish you'd believe me when I say your life is in great danger.

"Someone on your ranch is dealing with Cross, and if you don't find out who and put a stop to it, you don't stand a chance. You may not anyway.

"Why don't you go back down south to your people, Miss Houston? This is no place for a well-born lady like you. Go before this land is drenched in blood, and some of it yours." He turned on his heel and took great long strides toward the barn.

Charlie shouted after him. "I won't leave, this is where I belong. We've sent for the marshal."

Mitch raised his shoulders and halted. She was one stubborn woman. He gave it one more try, turning to face her. "Listen to me. The territorial marshal has more feuds and fusses to see after than can be handled in this country. Hell, it'd take two months just to ride over half of it. For the most part they'll let the vigilantes take care of justice in these parts, and you and I both know who controls the local vigilantes. As for the army, they've got their hands full fighting the Indians right now. You can expect nothing from them. What do they care about a small range war? The colonel has hired men who are nothing but wild animals running on instinct."

Trapped by a sudden inexplicable anger, Charlie ran toward Mitch. "And what are you, Fallon, but an animal?" she hissed.

The heat of her wrath washed over him like a brutal summer wind off the prairie, and he batted his eyes. He was surprised he didn't stumble backward under her attack. Instead he turned and strode briskly to the barn where he saddled the black and rode out, paying little attention to the direction in which he headed. It happened to be north, and it wasn't long before he came upon a herd of cattle carrying the Circle D brand. Reining the black's head to the right he swung back toward the east and the Double H Ranch. He might just manage to save Charlie Houston in spite of her bullheadedness.

Despite earlier plans to the contrary, Charlie rode back to the ranch after her disturbing meeting with Mitchell Fallon and the band of Cheyenne at Cal's ranch. The ever-faithful Ritter tagged along.

They rode on in silence for a while, Charlie contemplating the morning's happenings.

Finally she asked, "Do you put much stock in what Fallon said about someone at the Double H being in cahoots with the colonel?"

"Nah. I figgered he's just trying to draw attention away from his own self. We might have asked him just how come he showed up so quick after we found Zeke's body."

She nodded. "Or for that matter how come he's always conveniently around when something happens. You'd think a man working for the colonel would ride with the colonel's men, instead of hanging around my place all the time. Every time I turn around there he is." And sometimes in a most startling way, she thought but didn't say, remembering the night before when he'd literally walked out of fire.

Ritter studied her overlong. "Oh, is that right? Like when?"

Quietly she changed the subject. "Do you think the Indians are really going to fight?"

"I wouldn't be surprised. And I reckon it's time we done something about the problem. It don't seem to be possible to live side by side with them. They just keeping stealing cows and horses and ragging folks."

She reined in and gazed out across the rolling valley toward the distant peaks, shadows of purple and deep blue in the dusk. "Can't much blame them for wanting to keep this beautiful land."

"Nor us either," Ritter replied. "We might ought to get moving. If it's true what them braves said, there'll be war parties about. It wouldn't do to get caught out after dark."

Yancey Barton rode into the Double H late that same evening not long after Ritter and Charlie arrived. Ritter's version of Zeke's death, that the Indians had done it, and Charlie's vehement denial, were met with some ideas of his own.

"Now, Miss Charlie, you know you've been a mite partial to the red man. You sure you ain't giving him the benefit of the doubt."

All three had gathered eagerly around the cook fire to fill their plates with helpings of Crane's delicious rabbit strew. Charlie ate in silence and waited for Yancey to continue.

He did. "Ritter saw him scalped, plain as can be. It was some of them wild Cheyenne, no doubt about it. They've been off the reservation from over Dakota Territory for years now. And it sounds to me like it's all about to come to a head. They've got their backs against it, they'll turn and fight, and if you ask me it's about time the army took care of the problem once and for all."

She eyed him critically. "And you've always hated the Indian. He couldn't do anything right, as far as you're concerned."

"It's a known fact they ain't any good Indians less'n they're dead, and you know that. This country'll be better off when they're wiped out."

"What about the women, Yancey, and the babies? Little babies? How can you say that?"

"Those little babies grow up into big bad Indians that'd just as soon scalp you as look at you. Besides, it don't look like we'll have to worry overmuch too long. There's a lot of talk that the army is moving on them. They're coming up from Fort Fetterman and from out west at Fort Ellis. That foppish Custer will be in on it, you can bet. The government's fed up with dealing with these red savages breaking the law. They belong on a reservation or, better yet, dead."

A shudder passed through her and she stopped eating. Even the delicious stew didn't stand a chance against nightmarish visions of the massacre of families such as those she had visited in Spotted Moon's camp. It would be bloody and brutal and she hated to think about it. She hated too the way Yancey spoke of those people, as if they weren't even human, though it did echo how most white folks felt.

The more she thought about his words, the more upset she became. The idea that little Indian babies would soon be massacred by a bunch of soldiers armed to the teeth was too much to bear.

She decided to ride over and speak to Spotted Moon's family, try to talk them into going back up into Dakota Territory to the reservation before something terrible happened. It would be best not to tell Yancey or Ritter where she was going. She finished her meal, then went to the house.

Just before dawn, with the sky glowing a metallic silver not yet color-washed by the sun, she sneaked out the back door. She had staked Belle out in the scrub pine the night before so Ritter wouldn't spot her leaving and tag along. The way he felt about Indians, he would be no asset and might actually cause trouble for her. She left a note that she had gone to visit the McGrew and Burris ranches to the north to discuss the threat Colonel Dunkirk posed.

The day unfolded serenely in lavenders and pinks and golds and found Charlie well on her way. A gentle breeze stiffened as the sun came up, blowing from the southwest to caress her cheeks. A few times she thought she smelled smoke, but for the first few hours of her trip saw nothing but an occasional skittery rabbit, some distant high-flying birds, and a scurrying lizard. Along about noon she stopped for lunch near a spread of juniper thick with blueberries.

Mitch almost rode up on her out on the little rocky flat, but her roan kicked up some loose stones that warned him just in time to keep that from happening.

When she rode on he was not far behind. Where in God's name was she going?

During the afternoon the roan climbed a long, steady rise that topped out abruptly, the panorama below bringing Charlie to a halt. Across the wide expanse of rolling valley cut by the Little Bighorn River was camped the biggest gathering of Indians she'd ever seen.

Dear God, what were they up to?

She remembered what Spotted Moon had said, the words of war that she had taken almost lightly because she never truly believed the Indian would turn and fight when he saw the huge army of the white man. She'd always thought they would just pick away at isolated groups of whites, and eventually those that were left would settle peacefully on the reservations. But this. This was an army of Indians. Thousands of them. They were certainly not just a few Cheyenne families like she'd seen in the spring. It was a camp of gigantic proportions, the settlement sending up a pall of smoke that hung thick in the valley.

This time Mitch did ride up on her.

She jerked her mount's head around to confront him. "What in the hell name are you doing *still* following me around?"

Mouth open to reply, his glance moved beyond her shoulder and he said in hushed awe, "Oh, dear God."

The admiration in that uttering caused her to turn once again to behold the magnificent sight.

Black dread then struck him speechless. Here they were, the last of a magnificent people, finally pushed as far as they would push. Ready to fight, ready to die. His gut tingled with the fearful knowledge. He wanted to ride out across the prairie, waving his hat, shout a warning that they must leave, go back to the reservation where they would be safe. But all he could do was stare in total fascination at the mighty force.

Finally the spell was broken, and he nudged Jeb with his heels. It was as if he no longer even knew Charlie was there. He rode to the very rim of the rise and stood in the stirrups to get a better view.

"That Cheyenne was right, I guess," he said then, so softly she had to strain to hear him.

Haranguing him about following her would do no good, Charlie decided, so she asked, "Are those Cheyenne?"

"Lord, no. Well, maybe some, but you are looking at the biggest gathering of Sioux you'll probably ever see in one place in your lifetime, maybe ever. I'd bet Crazy Horse himself is down there, and the Hunkpapa chief, Gall. Aren't they magnificent?"

She dragged in a breath, trying to see what he saw. And yes, they were magnificent and quite terrifying.

Fearful of taking her eyes off the Indians she cast a quick look toward him. "How do you know so much about the Sioux?"

"My wife...." He didn't finish, but turned to meet her gaze with the same profound green expression she'd seen before. Like looking through moss into a bottomless pool of icy clear water.

"Wife?" She whispered the word and wet her lips, suddenly wanting a drink from the canteen hanging near her knee, but she couldn't look away from Mitchell Fallon. For he stared past the Indians into a place she sensed no longer existed, and whatever he was thinking eased the harsh lines of his rugged face into repose. The expression softened the definition of his lips so they were no longer drawn tight. He was thinking about someone he loved.

A bright memory struck her, of that full lower lip, moist and insistent against hers when he came at her out of that fire like some apparition. It had been like being seduced by the devil. But now, catching him in this unguarded moment, she remembered only the pure, intense pleasure. She felt herself flush and tried to cover the embarrassment with a question.

"What do you suppose they're up to?" she asked in a whisper. She wanted to say, *tell me about your wife*, but didn't.

"What?" He came away from wherever he'd been, once again the hard-bitten Mitchell Fallon. Tense, somber, and ready to face the enemy. "Waiting for the army, I'd say. Waiting to fight and die."

"Well, shouldn't we tell someone?"

"Who? God, look at that."

"Well, someone. They'll butcher them."

"They're ready for battle, no doubt about it."

"Fallon, listen to me. We can't let the army ride into this."

"Why not?" He spat out the words. "This is their last chance, don't you see that? Why would we want to ruin it for them? Let them have what little glory there is left. Let them die in an honorable way without our interference, not starve to death on some damned reservation."

"There are so many of them. You're talking as if the Indian will lose. How can you think that, with so many of them down there? And what's honorable about dying?" Charlie's horse danced sideways and she gentled her.

"What's honorable about stealing their land and sending them to live in some godforsaken place that we'll take away from them soon enough if we see fit?"

She opened her mouth to argue some more before she realized that he was voicing her opinions, the ones she'd come to Montana with, the ones her father had espoused, the ones she'd only yesterday been using against Ritter and Yancey. Why should she argue with Mitchell Fallon just because of who he was?

"I'd always hoped we could all live here," she said, and spread one arm wide so that the roan half stepped again. "There's so much land. So much. Just look at how much."

He laughed, a brutal, hard sound that grated on her ears. "White men can't even get along with each other. We just fought a war, brother against brother, because we couldn't get along.

"And them down there. Hell, they fight with each other all the time over one thing or another. What makes you think we can live side by side with an entirely different culture? Best to get it over and done with, not prolong the agony. They'll meet their destiny just like we'll one day meet ours."

She gaped. A man like him, speaking of destiny and scruples. She'd never expected it.

"Well, I'm going to ride down to... to...."

"Leave it be. You don't even know if the army is on its way. That idiot Custer wouldn't believe you if you could find him and warn him."

"Yancey came back last night, he said Custer is riding in with troops, and some others too."

He shrugged. "We could stay and watch. It'll be a fine battle."

"How can you be so cold?"

"Cold? I watched my Sioux wife die because there wasn't a white man in town who would stand up for her, nor me when I tried to save her. Why in hell should I care what happens to a few soldiers. If they'd done their jobs, this wouldn't be happening in the first place.

"Now, I'd suggest if you don't want to get caught up in this mess, you'd better just ride away." Green fire flashed from his eyes that were no longer peaceful or still.

She took up her reins in one hand. Fallon's wife was dead, and he had loved her. "And is that what you're going to do too? Just ride away?"

"No, Miss Houston, I think I'll ride on down there and join the Indians. Might be fun to see how many whites I can kill before one gets me."

"You're mad, stark raving mad."

"Probably," he said, then rose in his stirrups and whacked the huge black stallion across the rump.

Tears filled her eyes as she watched the man and horse tear down the incline in a straight, unwavering line toward the encampment of Sioux. She wanted to follow, she wanted to shout at him not to go, not to die, but all she could do was swallow past a dry lump in her throat and watch a trail of dust follow him across the rolling prairie toward the camp. It was only later that she thought she never did find out what he was doing following her, but by then it didn't seem to matter.

He found Celia's brothers in the camp, the two of them painted for war in brilliant streaks that disguised the amiable natures he had always known in these men. Across their stoic faces slashes of black and red made of them brutal savages, just like the white men believed they were. Mitch knew better, but he found his brothers-in-law far past caring about anything but this one final encounter.

Though they spoke of destroying the white man once and for all, Mitch sensed beneath their words of bravado the knowledge that this would simply begin their own destruction. They had no idea of how bad it would get before it was over. Perhaps he didn't either.

He bid them farewell just as night fell, embracing each in turn and saying the words Celia had taught him, the words that had no translations to the white man's tongue. He would meet them again in another place, where the spirits guarded his wife and child at this very moment.

When he rode away, the taste of futility lay on his tongue like ashes from the cold fires of another time.

Eleven

Tim Lawrence, one of Duffy McGrew's hands, raced in on a lathered horse, leaping off before the animal came to a full halt. Charlie was down at the corral watching Ritter work with an unbroken bronco. The sound of pounding hoof-beats raised goose bumps across her shoulders. The way things had been going she expected the worst. Someone else must be dead.

Even as she and Ritter ran to meet the man, she dreaded to hear what he had to say. Nothing could have prepared her for the horrible news.

"It's them savages. They've done killed the army. Custer's dead, they're all dead. My God, you should see it. Dead soldiers and dead Indians and dead horses, all piled everywhere, and this one lone horse standing in the middle of it. Just standing there like he didn't know what happened. Leather Norse from the Burris ranch rode up on it. Says he could still hear the blasts of gunfire echoing in the air. Me, I doubt that, but you know old Leather.

"Army's got the rest of them savages pinned down, or vice versa, who knows. Leather, he didn't stick around to find out. He lit out, you can bet he did, soon as he seen it. Plumb turned his stomach, and him at Bull Run too."

Her knees wobbled, threatened to buckle, and she grabbed

Ritter's arm for support. She couldn't speak as the boy put his hands on his knees and gasped for air so he could go on.

"The rest is coming," he panted.

She shot a look of panic toward Ritter.

The young man grabbed the lanky rider's arm. "What do you mean, Indians are coming? Are they going to kill us all?"

"No... *no*. The army, a whole 'nother column of 'em riding south down the Bighorn," he said. "Goin' to finish them Sioux off. Ever' last one of 'em. So Leather said. Word is they're gonna kill the Indians till they ain't a one left, not man, woman, nor child. They massacred Custer and the Seventh. What do you expect? It was Gall, they say. Gall and Crazy Horse."

She remembered Fallon mentioning both names. She wondered if he was still at the Sioux camp when it happened. And everyone dead. Surely that wasn't right. All those families, women and babies. Dear God in heaven. Spotted Moon's child, the child she'd held in her arms, kissed the soft cheek, nuzzled the soft down of his dear head. Tears rolled silently down her cheeks. She wanted desperately for someone to put their arms around her, comfort her. It was hard sometimes to be strong.

A shiver passed through her, and she straightened, turned back to the issue at hand, and tried to quiet the boy.

"Settle down, that's enough. Somebody, take this man's horse to the barn and cool him off."

While one of the hands who had raced up to hear most of the story led the horse away, Charlie and Ritter took the excited young man to the porch steps, sat him down, and fetched him a cool dipper of water.

Tim swallowed a few gulps, shook his head. "You shoulda seen it. My God." He drank some more. "A bunch of us rode on down there first thing this morning. Lord, I ain't never seen nothing like it in all my borned days."

The boy was all of seventeen, and the remark under other circumstances would have been humorous. But uttered thusly in the midst of such heartrending news, it only served to sound poignant.

"Well," she said after a moment. "I guess they got what they wanted." She tried not to think again of the innocent victims of such senseless violence.

"What?" Ritter asked vaguely.

"Oh, just something someone said to me about the Indians dying honorably in battle rather than starving on some reservation."

Ritter made a rude noise and went to refill the water dipper.

Nervous chatter finally muted, Tim hugged his knees and stared off into space, contemplating the horrific scene he'd witnessed.

"Did you know Mitchell Fallon?" she asked, and tried to keep her tone noncommittal.

"Who?"

"That gunslinger Colonel Dunkirk hired. The one with the white stripe in his hair."

"Don't reckon I did, ma'am," Tom said in a trembly voice. "Heard talk of him, though. Why?"

She gazed off in the direction of the Little Big Horn. Dear God, suppose he had meant what he said and had remained with the Sioux and been killed? But then the boy said it was Custer and his men who were all slain. Some of the Indians survived, at least till the rest of the army caught up with them. Well, it was useless to worry. After all, there was no reason for her to have an interest in the fate of a gunslinger. Was there?

She got up from the step and walked out across the dusty yard hugging herself. Tears filled her eyes once again and she let the warm drops run unheeded down her cheeks. Oh, the stupidity of it all. Men and their deadly games.

Ritter caught up with her before she reached the barn. "Miss Charlie? Tim there, he's plumb tuckered and no one has rode to tell the rest of the ranchers hereabouts, just them up north. I think someone should ride out. Tim says that Leather wanted him to ride on to Miles City, see what news there is of the army."

She lowered her head, keeping it turned away from him while she wiped her wet cheeks. "And you want to do it?"

"Yes. Well, I mean, someone should. It's not like I'd be leaving you here alone. There's Slate and P.J. and Crane in case something happens."

She chuckled bitterly. "If those Indians decide to massacre every white man in this territory, no two or three cowboys will stop them. You know what? I think I'll just ride with you. Let the boys watch over the place. We can ride back out tomorrow. I'm curious too just what's going on other places. Let's get saddled up."

For once, Ritter didn't object like he usually did when she made her own decisions. He just nodded and went with her to the corral to fetch a couple of horses. They wouldn't, after all, be riding anywhere near the battle. Ritter wished he could ride out and watch awhile, and he might just do that once he got Miss Charlie safe in Miles City. This idea of hers was a good one. For a change, he wouldn't have to watch every move she made to keep her safe. Wonder she didn't want to ride out and watch the army whip them red savages. She clearly had something else on her mind, though.

It was late before they arrived in Miles City, though they didn't tarry at any of their stops to warn sodbusters and ranchers along the route. The town was crowded and afire with the wildest of rumors.

They tied their horses at a crowded hitching rail and Charlie went to see if she could find a place to spend the night. Ritter headed for the Powder Keg, which was bulging so that he could hardly shove his way through the swinging doors.

Bits and pieces of conversation bounced around as he made his way to the bar, dodging an occasional elbow or boot heel or sloshing beer mug.

"Hear tell they massacred every white from Dakota Territory all the way here."

"Man ain't safe in his own bed when a whole army can't stop a few piddling red savages."

"Few. Few? Some say they was ten thousand of them out there, hiding and laying in wait, and Custer, that idjit who can't find his own behind to put on his pants, just rode right into it. Him and fifty men."

"Fifty? I heard more like three hundred and fifty."

"Well, I ain't gonna go count the bodies. Are you?"

"Guess they got back at him for Sand Creek, huh?"

"And the Washita too."

"Them was Cheyenne."

"Well, fool, they's Cheyenne with them Sioux. Been here awhile, just waiting."

Ritter ordered a whiskey and leaned on the bar.

The town was a beehive of activity. The excitement of the battle between Custer and the Sioux had sure brought everyone running. Charlie wondered how long it would take to get something to eat and headed up the street. If nothing else, she'd buy something in the general store, if there was anything left.

Mitchell Fallon hadn't joined the crowd at the Powder Keg Saloon. When word reached Miles City of Custer's defeat at the hands of Gall and Crazy Horse and all those Sioux and Cheyenne, he had spent some time riding the trail alone under the vast dark sky.

It was a warm, sensuous night, the kind of night created especially for speaking to the spirit world. He'd never had much of a religion before Celia, and she hadn't ragged him about it. Just demonstrated her own beliefs in a quiet and peaceful way that made him envy her. Once she grew large with child, she began to talk to the unborn baby, explaining her gods, and Mitchell finally understood her serenity. He never was sure he believed, but he did learn to understand. Perhaps that's all that kept him sane when she and the baby were killed, if indeed he was sane. Sometimes he thought himself quite mad.

He rode on into Miles City Monday evening, searching for word of what the army would do. All anyone learned was that the battle raged on, with Major Reno and Captain Benteen's forces pinned down by the surviving Sioux and Cheyenne. He considered riding out and joining the battle, but he was too white for the Sioux to accept, and he couldn't raise up arms against his wife's clan. So he waited and watched.

Late in the evening he saw Charlie riding out of town all alone, and he tagged along. Where her shadow had got to he had no idea. She probably took off when he wasn't looking.

Dark found Charlie making camp a little ways out of town near the river in a small clearing surrounded by thick box elder and sandbar willow. After unsaddling Belle and staking her out in some grass nearby, she rustled up some kindling and built a fire. Spreading her bedroll near the crackling fire, she sat, dug a Barlow from her pocket, and tackled a can of peaches.

A rider approached as she speared up the first sweet golden piece of fruit. She dropped knife and peach half back in the can and grabbed up her Winchester from where it rested against a log. In the excitement she kicked over the can of peaches, but came around just in time to point the weapon at Mitchell Fallon's midsection.

Though relief poured through her at seeing him alive, she yelled at him anyway. "*Damn* you, Fallon. You made me spill my peaches. I thought you'd be dead."

He stood beside his horse, holding the reins. "You going to shoot me with that thing, or just point it at me?"

She put the rifle down and grabbed up the can. All the juice had run out, but some of the fruit remained. She tried to concentrate on eating, wishing she could ignore his presence entirely. But her heart thumped hard against her chest, and she didn't think it was from fear. She had truly been afraid that he had died in yesterday's battle, or maybe been wounded badly. Relief at seeing him alive and in one piece poured through her, a surprising, palpable emotion. He looked perfectly okay, now that she had a chance to check him out.

While she entertained all these thoughts Fallon had let his horse's reins drop to the ground and hunkered down by the fire, making himself at home just like he belonged there.

"Hoping you'd have come coffee."

"Well, I don't."

"You've got some peaches," he said, and grinned quite suddenly and unexpectedly.

She liked what it did to his features. The corners of his eyes and mouth lifted, dimples broke the severe angularity of his cheeks, nicely even teeth flashed, and his green eyes sparkled an intriguing fire all their own.

As if he had her in some kind of spell she held out the can. "Have some. It was all they had left in the store. We'll be hungry in five minutes." The double meaning didn't escape her.

Nor him, obviously, considering the lustful grin he displayed. "Thank you, I believe I will." He moved closer, picked out the knife she'd left standing in the can, and stabbed out a half. Without taking his eyes off her he gingerly slid the fruit onto his tongue. Sweet juice glimmered on his lips. His throat rippled when he swallowed and he handed her the knife and then the can so that she had to touch his warm fingers.

"Thank you kindly," he said, and his tongue flicked out to lick away the juice.

She watched with fascination, overcome with a powerful urge to kiss those sticky sweet lips. Heat swarmed up her throat and into the roots of her hair. Fallon took off his hat, leaned back on the log where she'd propped her rifle, and sighed.

"Thank you," he repeated, and closed his eyes.

"You said that." Her voice broke and she had to search for it again before continuing. She almost forgot what she was going to ask him, then she remembered. "What are you doing? Why do you turn up everywhere I go?"

"What? Me?" He didn't open his eyes. "Right now trying to get some shut-eye."

"Here?" She forgot that he hadn't answered her most important question. Why he kept following her.

He let his eyelids drift open languidly and pinned her with an amused stare. "Public property. Doesn't belong to anyone in particular."

She studied him for a long while. "You're awfully unconcerned considering what happened to your friends."

"What happened to my friends?"

Surely he knew. "Well, a lot of them died yesterday, and more are going to, I'd guess."

"They counted a lot of coup. They killed that bastard Custer, they won their battle. And it's not unconcern, it's a harmony of sorts. What I am sorry about is that it won't last. You're right, by this time tomorrow, the tide will probably turn, but at least they will have honored their forefathers."

She sighed. "I don't understand."

He sat up, looked at her intently. "I know, but you don't have to." He heaved himself to his feet. "Well, if you don't want me here, guess I'd better ride on." Raking back the long black hair he settled the hat on his head.

"Don't go," she said in a whisper.

"I didn't hear you," he replied, and leaned down close.

She cleared her throat and looked up at him, eyes reflecting orange flickers of flame from the campfire. "I said, don't go."

He nodded. "Ah."

He wanted to take her in his arms, throw her on the ground, and rip those stupid britches and shirt from her body, reveal the true woman that she was. A full-grown, healthy woman. He wanted to teach her what that body was really made for, and it wasn't busting broncs and riding herd on some stubborn longhorns. It wasn't trying to hang on to land so rough it would kill her long before her time. It would dry her up, wear her out and kill her, if some terrible disease or crazy Indian or whiskey-soaked cowboy didn't do it first.

Instead he knelt on the ground very close to her so that he could smell her hair and her skin, her breath sweet as the peaches they'd shared. And he put one hand up to the side of her face and rubbed her cheek with a thumb.

She didn't expect the sudden gesture, but she remained very still, wanting badly for him to take her in his arms. Her breasts tingled with the desire and she licked her lips. He bent forward quickly, captured the tip of her tongue between his lips, and held her like that an instant, moaning softly, waiting for her response. She opened her mouth to him, and he laced the fingers of one hand through her hair, holding her close, tight, lips locked to his.

She put one arm around his neck, the other along his shoulder, and he lifted her so that her aching breasts pressed tightly against his chest.

The inside of his mouth was soft and moist and peach-flavored, and his tongue did things that nearly drove her mad before he moved to lapping and kissing down across her jawbone and to the sensitive flesh below her ear. His hat tumbled off bouncing on her shoulder, and then he had her on the ground, lying beside her. At her back the warmth of the fire did not even compete with the heat of her desire.

His hungry mouth searched past the collar of the shirt, then he ripped it away, buttons popping off. She wore a light undershirt and her nipples were rigid against the fabric, rising and falling with the gasping of her breath. He took one in his mouth, wetting the thin cotton and exploding an exquisite pain within her that spread from far down in her belly and filled her body with bright wonder. Her head swam with intense pleasure and she reached out for him, fingers pushing up his shirt so she could span the taut muscles with spread hands. Life breathed beneath her palms, vibrant and warm.

He grabbed the hem of her undershirt, tugged it up to kiss her belly just above the belt of her jeans, then fumbled with the buckle. It didn't budge. Frustrated, he grunted and got on his knees astraddle of her, turning her so that she lay on her back looking up at him.

"Oh, Mitch. I've never… oh, please, just… I can't."

The buckle came loose under his fumbling fingers. "Help me. Undo these buttons. Hurry." He kissed her bared breast, his tongue playing around the nipple until she cried out in ecstasy.

How could anything feel so good? She writhed, moaned when his lips left her breast so he could go back to work on the buttons of her jeans.

Dragging in several deep breaths, she put her hands flat across the front of her pants. She wanted him, wanted him desperately, but she couldn't let this happen. Not now, and not this way. This wild, untamed outlaw would get what he wanted and ride off. Then what would become of her? Oh, dear God, all she wanted was him inside her.

"No. You've got to stop. I can't... *we* can't. Oh, please. I'm sorry. I can't."

He panted, tried to push her hands aside. "You what? You can't? Of course you can. It's easy, just close your eyes and make a wish. It won't hurt, you're strong. I won't hurt you, I won't."

"But I've never... never before... I can't just do it like this. Please, Fallon. This is crazy. I want you too, but... dammit, *stop*!"

She struggled, slapped at him ineffectually, rolled her head around. All she wanted was to be in his arms, to enclose him within her aching loins, feel his mouth on hers, his tongue doing all those wild things to her. And he seemed to sense it so that she couldn't stop him.

The crazy desire fueled her anger. This was *wrong*. She'd be sorry and so would he, then he would be gone and then where would she be. Where was love? No, she'd never find love. This... this was simply raw, unbridled lust.

All of a sudden, she realized he had stopped trying to undo her pants. He still knelt over her, but his hands were resting on the ground on either side of her while he breathed raggedly, his head hanging down so that his hair tickled at her cheek.

She touched his face tenderly, held away the hair so she could see his green eyes, smoky with passion. "I'm so sorry."

He took a deep breath, moved imperceptibly away from her touch. "Yeah, me too."

He took his time getting off her, as if hoping she might change her mind and they could go on. But he didn't push it and when she lay stiffly, not saying anything more, he dragged in the night air once, twice, then leaned back against the log. She could hear the rasp of his heavy breathing.

The shirt wouldn't button back up, he'd torn off all the buttons, so she tied it at her waist, extremely conscious of the wet spot on the undershirt where he had sucked at her breast through the cotton fabric. A cavity deep down in her belly throbbed with heat and dissatisfaction.

They both watched the fire till he finally threw a couple of sticks on it and said, "Why didn't you tell me you... I mean, a woman your age, I just thought...."

Miserably she shook her head. "Yeah, well, you can just think something else. And why would it have been all right if I'd had a man before?"

"I didn't mean it that way. I just meant... oh, hell, I don't know what I meant. We haven't got any business messing around with each other anyway."

"My feelings exactly. That's why I stopped you, not because I've never... never made love. Nothing could come of it, and I don't want to let you think it could. And I certainly don't want to let a man have me who's just going to ride away."

"Trouble is," he said with a wry grin, "if I stick around it's bound to happen again. You see, I can't seem to keep my eyes or thoughts off you. Not ever since I saw you dancing that night, graceful as a white dove."

"Saw me dancing? When did you—?"

He interrupted as if she hadn't spoken. "God, you are so beautiful, and you keep yourself hid in those ugly clothes so no one will guess what you've got there." He pointed in the general direction of her chest.

She spread her hands over her breasts, imagining him spying on her in those most private of moments. "You've been peeping in my windows, spying on me? How could you do something like that? Even you?"

He raised an eyebrow. "Even me? Oh, you mean a man

with no scruples, a man who goes around shooting people? That kind of man?"

"That's exactly what I mean. I guess I shouldn't be surprised at anything you'd do."

He gazed at her. A look of sadness came over his face and he reached out a crooked finger, ran it down her bare flesh in the gap of her unbuttoned shirt. "Well, maybe I would do just about anything, but I didn't... I wouldn't ever do anything to hurt you. I'd like you to believe that. Don't ask me why it matters, but it does."

She remained very still, though doing so took every ounce of her energy. He'd become in her mind no longer a bloodthirsty gunfighter, but a man seeking her approval, courting her in some odd sort of way. Not the kind of courting that offers up the live-happily-ever-after fairy-tale ending, but a promise of mutual trust, of friendship.

She found herself wishing he were someone else, then immediately thought that wasn't right, for if he were he would have no appeal for her. He had a tough inner strength and she liked to think she did too. Both had been scarred but surely not irrevocably.

Without hesitation, she cupped a hand around his fingers, still trailing languidly down the front of the open shirt, and lifted them to her lips.

Transfixed, he kept his eyes on her, unsure what to expect. First she said yes, then no, now was it yes again? He waited, desire for her growing once more. This time, maybe they wouldn't stop.

She lifted her head, gave him back his hand. "I'd like it if you would stay here tonight. It was foolish of me to come out here alone, considering what's going on."

Hope erupted from deep down in his gut, but then he

looked into her eyes, like great black marbles shining in the firelight. And he saw there sorrow, regret.

"Just that?" he asked softly.

She nodded.

"Fine. You're right about it... us... being foolish, but I don't expect you'll change your ways anytime soon, and from what I've seen you're an expert at foolish."

"Now you're mad at me."

He chuckled grimly. "Hell, yes, I'm mad at you. If it weren't for you I'd be halfway to Idaho right now."

"I don't see that as very desirable. And how did I keep you from going to Idaho?"

"By being so stubborn, that's how. Why don't you sell out and go back home? What in thunder is wrong with you, woman?"

She cringed at the term. "Woman? *Woman?* I'm not woman, I'm *me*, Charlie Houston. I don't call you *man*. And I won't sell out, I'll never sell out. My daddy sacrificed his life for his dream, and if you think I'm going to give it up, you're crazy."

He nodded and leaned back on the log, staring into the fire. "And what is your dream, Charlie Houston?"

She opened her mouth to answer, the automatic reply that had always come so easily before she'd met this man. That her father's dream and hers were the same, but she didn't get the words said. Things had happened to make her think about that.

All she finally said was, "I don't know, Fallon. I guess I just don't know anymore."

Velda Brotherton writes from her home perched on the side of a mountain against the Ozark National Forest. Branded as *Sexy, Dark and Gritty*, her work embraces the lives of gutsy women and heroes who are strong enough to deserve them. After a stint writing for a New York publisher, she has settled comfortably in with small publishers to produce novels in several genres.

Facebook: Author Velda Brotherton
Twitter: @veldabrotherton
www.veldabrotherton.com